Ghost Talk

A Short Story Collection from the Unsettled Souls Series

By

Foyle Ravenstead

Published by Unchained Pen Ltd
ᴏ⪡◊⪢ᴏ

93 Green Lane, Chichester
PO19 7NU, United Kingdom

A CIP catalogue record for this book is available from the
British Library.

ISBN: 978-1-910304-18-1

Contents

When They Light the Candle 1

Undying Love at the Trullo..31

Mary McKinnon: Launched into Eternity..................69

Connie's Blind Love 111

Deauville du Coup..161

When They Light the Candle

Epigraph

Those who have suffered understand suffering
and therefore extend their hand.

Patti Smith

Chapter One

Of all the places I could have been, my sister's house was least preferable, for I was the uninvited guest and the one they'd rather not have.

It was the time of the modern plague, Covid. No doctor would come out to me, and it was too dangerous to go to A&E, as hospitals were a hive for the new and apocalyptic bug.

My little one, Christopher, was at war with a fever. Roasting like a turkey in an oven, he was too hot to speak or even open his eyes. He'd been falling in and out of consciousness, in a delirium that frightened me to the core. He was lost in the battle, rarely acknowledging me, and I was scared that he wouldn't make his second birthday at the end of the month.

There's no father to help me with the nursing, because he's as anonymous as he's unknown. Once, I had defiantly cheered that fact as an outward expression of my feminist perspective, but my political ambition has been dampened by the practicalities of parenting a young child: loss of income, a good night's sleep, and the sanity that comes with a social life. But I do have a sister and when Christopher fell ill, that's where we took refuge.

It was convenient. She lives in the same town, up on the hill, in Rancton Hall. It's one of the oldest houses in town, and I'm surprised they haven't turned it into a National Trust property.

It would have been easier if she'd just visited me once a day. All I needed was the daily reprieve of a cooked meal, a couple of hours to sleep and for her take a turn at the physicality of keeping Christopher clean. But Sophie insisted I came to her, and I didn't have the energy to negotiate.

I was sat on the same chair, where I had been sitting for days, a prisoner to the spot. The house was deathly quiet, as my sister, her husband and their daughter were asleep. I was lost in my thoughts, and believe me, they were not good company. I removed the flannel from Christopher's forehead and dipped it in a bowl of cool water, squeezed, then replaced it. How could I get him cooler?

We had the same parents, Sophie and I, but little else in common. She married the Reverend Colin Skippen and overnight became devout, socially responsible and as boring as hell. Decamping to hers meant moving to the rectory, which some would describe as a to-die-for mansion because it comes with all the middle-class charm of sash windows, servant bells and bug filled cellars. I just smell the damp. At least it didn't come with a churchyard. Who'd want to be near all those dead people? It did, however, come with all the sanctimonious piety and patriarchal tradition of a priest's house. It meant being beholden to Colin, reining in my potty mouth and participating in grace at supper time.

They'd given me the guest room, the one where a former priest is supposed to have died from the plague, all on his own. His body rotted away for months because no one was brave enough to collect it. I'd heard this plague story several times: once from a parishioner, once from a neighbour and then, the most entertaining in its telling, from the cleaner. The general theme was that the priest was in love with a servant woman and would not replace her when she died, hence finally dying on his own.

It's disconcerting being in his old bedroom as he's supposed to appear as a pustulated corpse, lying next to you as you sleep. But I shouldn't complain; at least I'm not in the attic where the boy haunts.

Most of the rooms have stories attached to them, of ethereal beings, malignant patients or curious tenants. An ancient house is bound to have stories, some of them real, some of them mythologised, where the full facts are unknown or forgotten. It's been a house at the centre of a community where people did religion and came for solace, so it will have such stories. I was just one more needy resident looking for refuge.

I'm very lucky that Sophie's taken me in. After all, no one can be sure Christopher's bug isn't Covid. But the bigger difficulty was Colin and me — our history. We've always been chalk and cheese. I'm the original rebel and would have protested on Greenham Common, if I'd been old enough at the time. I would have been arrested in the Poll Tax riots, if I hadn't been on holiday. I would have laid in the road with Extinction Rebellion, if I hadn't had to mother Christopher.

But this is the tip of the iceberg. Colin's Conservative, I'm Labour. He went to Cambridge, I did Bristol. He and Sophie were married at twenty-two, and they're each other's first love. I'm not quite sure who Christopher's father is. Well, it's one of two…, probably. The Skippens of Rancton House are God fearing, I'm not so sure. I'm not against the idea; I think it quite charming, and it gives me a warm feeling. But I'm not holding my breath for my soul to be saved. I fried that chance when I put salt in my dad's tea. The first time was a mistake, the next was after he withdrew my pocket money. Then there was the throwing of red gloss paint over my geography teacher's car—he shouldn't have looked at me that way. A lower point was when I posted one of my poos in the post box, after my dad sent money and a supportive letter to the BNP. Maybe all these are easily forgivable, but the event that led to Colin and I refusing to be in the same room for four years is the toughest to excuse. I announced to the local pub's patrons that Colin did porn every night. I was drunk, and I didn't expect anyone to believe me, let alone remember it the next day.

Colin calls himself a priest, but he's probably just a deacon, helping at the service by handing out the bread—the little wafers. I refused to be confirmed as I'd seen the pantomime of my brother's; the stupid costume, the pomp and ceremony and the very idea of 'this is my body, this is my blood.' Yuck, that's disgusting. I've only ever said that to my aunt and she made me promise never to say it again. I hadn't meant to be offensive.

Anyway, the church got to hear about my 'revelation' at the pub. Colin was called and questioned and that was when we stopped speaking. I did write a letter for him to give to his boss, the bishop or whatever, but Colin was mighty annoyed. He should have forgiven me straight away, it's what he's supposed to do. My sister did. No one in the pub was interested anyway. They knew I was joking.

Having to ask for my sister's support now, for refuge in the rectory, was a milestone. To be fair, Colin did welcome me on the doorstep with a hug, carried my bags up and didn't mention the pub episode. It was like nothing had ever happened. I like it when people do that. People should always do that.

Christopher sighed and reached out for my hand. It was boiling hot. I wondered whether I should take his temperature again. But it was so frightening every time I did it. How could it be so high? No, I should do it. I searched amongst my detritus for the thermometer. I'd

5

turned the guest room, which doubles up as Colin's office, into a war zone. There had been no time to keep it tidy.

It's not a real rectory, just an old house, and it's nearly half a mile to the church. There's a weird old headstone in the garden, but I'm pretty sure there's nothing underneath it. It's decorated with some Latin words: omnis, qui credit in ipsum, something, something, but that doesn't make it a grave. Okay, there's another short stone in front, but there's only like two feet between them, so if it was a foot stone, the body would have to be ridiculously short. Maybe it even predates the house. Or maybe it's one of those Victorian curiosities they liked to cheer the landscape up with.

But the house is miserably old and must have had some leaning to the Catholic faith because it has a proper priest hole. It's halfway up the stairs to the attic, not a hole as such, more of a cupboard. There's a tiny vent that lets in five round beams of light, but I wouldn't want to be in there for more than a second, well not for longer than you can hold your breath, as it smells like the last occupant left something behind. It's behind a hidden door in the panelling; you lift a bit of trim, and it opens. You can lock yourself in, which Colin does as a party trick. He goes inside and proves that you can't get in once he's locked it. The trim doesn't even move. Unfortunately, there's not a lock on the outside to keep him in there.

The attic ghost actually comes as two entities: the Bird Lady and the boy. But it's only the boy that does the haunting. The Bird Lady is only called The Bird Lady because she spoke to the birds. I think it was because she was French, and no one could or would speak with her. She'd fallen in love with a sailor and followed him back to England. But when she arrived, he disowned her after their first night of passion. Some say he had to sail for Spain. Either way, she was effectively abandoned, and not having a couple of ducats to rub together, she was all at sea.

Being French didn't go down well with the locals, what with all the wars between our nations and being Catholic. The anti-popery sentiment, very common at the time, made life problematic. She was without a trade, a family or a reputation, and was probably the most unwanted person in the parish, the town, maybe even the county.

Her solution was to become a nun. There was a Catholic convent nearby, it's a school now. Roman Catholicism was fading fast and furious on account of Henry VIII having fallen out with the Pope. So, having failed in love, she was all set for a life of marriage to God. But the consequences of her night of passion with the sailor ruined this saving grace. When the convent found out she was pregnant they asked her to leave. Fortunately, the local priest wanted some help at his rectory, and being destitute she took the job gratefully. She bore a son who she called François. Of all the names she could have chosen! He was far from incognito.

It was all going fine until the Parish Council found out the child wasn't registered and they didn't want to take the risk that she'd take advantage of the poor relief. They decided the boy must leave the parish.

She ducked and dived for a few months but in the end, they came knocking on the door: the sheriff and a couple of heavies. She hid her boy in the priest hole and, after three hours, they gave up searching. Tragically, when she called out to François to open the door, there was no answer, and the priest helped the Bird Lady to break in. They found François kneeling with his hands together in prayer, blue with cold and not breathing. As much as she tried to warm him with her hugs and kisses, she could not revive him. He had died, probably from fear. Maybe in the dark, François couldn't find the latch to open the door, after all, he was only about three. Colin wants to dismantle this feature so you can't lock yourself in.

Christopher turned his head in agony from the fever. What could I do? Thoughts circled wildly through my mind. At what stage do I turn to prayer? If I resort to prayer now, then I am helpless, I only have hope and I will not place reliance on something beyond my control.

I could hear the house waking up. It started with the laughter of four-year-old Ottilie, running down the hall. She has such a wonderful laugh.

For a long time I'd never wanted a child, not through all my twenties. There were too many downsides: the responsibilities, the cost, the commitment. The upside was unknown and uncertain, as I'd always seen my Mum suffer. Did she ever get to have a life? But when Ottilie was born, it changed my mind. Well, actually, it was when Ottilie began to speak that I was convinced.

Although I wasn't seeing Colin, Sophie made sure that I kept in contact with Ottilie. She never said that was her plan, but whenever I saw her, Ottilie was there, and Sophie would find a hundred and one excuses for me to engage with Ottilie. I'd babysit: I needed the money. We'd play: it was a giggle. I'd take Ottilie to the park: it got me out of the house.

Ottilie is the original indigo child, alert, creative and intuitive, and spending time with her triggered all those maternal instincts and longing that's inconvenient when you're single.

It took ages to get pregnant as I didn't have a regular boyfriend, and the casuals were all really careful, even when I said I was on the pill.

It was last Christmas that I saw Ottilie's true indigo quality. She was an early speaker and reader, and socially enthusiastic. Exhausting really, but so charming and easy to be with. We were on the carpet, Ottilie, Christopher and I. Christopher was not quite walking then. Sophie was in my kitchen making Sunday lunch. Ottilie turned to me and with the poignancy and articulation of a ten-year-old said "Christopher will be like a brother to me, and because I'm so young I will know him all my life. We'll be like you and Mummy, strong together." I was speechless.

Back at Christopher's bedside, I could hear Colin and Sophie talking quietly at the end of the hall, and shortly after Sophie came into the room.

'Kirsty I'm sorry, but we didn't know Christopher would take so long to recover.'

Here we go, I'm on my way home.

Sophie made a placating face, 'I need to move you to the attic. Colin is busy writing an important sermon and needs his office. He needs to concentrate and finish it.'

'No worries, that's fine. So, I'm going from Priest ghost to Attic Boy ghost.'

'He's got to keep working, sorry, even if it is a sermon delivered on Zoom.'

Sophie felt Christopher's forehead and fussed over his bedclothes.

Oh dear! The attic. It's grim up there and creepy.

'I've forgotten,' I said, 'what happened to the attic boy's mother, after he died?' I wanted Sophie to know what I'd be worrying about.

'Mademoiselle Oiseau? There are various versions; that she was tried for being a witch, which is frankly ridiculous; that she walks the corridors of the old school looking for him, which doesn't fit as the school was built two hundred years after he died. We think she was allowed to remain at Rancton because the Parish Council felt so guilty.'

'Guilty? Or were they avoiding bad publicity?'

'She was famous for standing by the stove and drinking tea nonstop, mourning the loss of her boy and beating herself up for having put him in the cupboard. She went back to the convent for a few months but couldn't throw off her grief and depression. In the end she returned to Rancton Hall, to be closer to where she'd lived with her son. She died a few years later from a broken heart.'

'Hmm, isn't that just old fashioned for suicide?'

I moved the eiderdown, an ancient bed linen and who, I wondered, had it once covered? Who knows how many had been nursed under it and what diseases they'd had? 'I didn't realise you knew so much more about the French woman.'

'Colin found an old book of letters in the church records.'

'Wow, you should have said.' This was exciting. 'So, it started when she fell in love with a sailor?'

'Yes, but it's not at all romantic. He was put ashore on a looting expedition, near Bordeaux. But when he broke into her house he was diverted from his mission and made love to the girl he was supposed to take advantage of. He stayed for hours and ended up telling her his home port. After he sailed off, she set off on her own journey, to England, to be with him.'

'Sassy!'

'Hmm, or foolish. It was okay for the first night. But the next day his friends hazed him for hooking up with a French woman. It didn't help when she protested at them loudly in French and shook her fist.'

'Good girl.'

'Not at all, he told her to leave.'

I was silenced as I imagined the Bird Lady abandoned and humiliated. So much pain, no wonder she haunts. I contemplated sleeping in the attic room that night. It's a simple room, off a narrow stairwell. The stairs have no carpet and there's barely any plaster on the wall, just some ancient shabby panelling. The attic room is equally decrepit.

'This house is so creepy, how do you put up with it? I mean, doesn't the mere knowledge that the priest died of plague revolt you? Possibly in this bed.'

Sophie gave me her annoying sisterly stare. 'No. There's never been plague in this house. He died of a broken heart. He was besotted with Mademoiselle Oiseau, but their love was forbidden.'

'Hmm, forbidden? Sounds kind of kinky.' I giggled. 'Who forbade it?'

'A priest was expected to be celibate.'

'Eh! What about you and Colin?'

'We were already married before he wanted to be ordained, so that was okay.'

Ooh, this was almost gossipy, and Sophie doesn't do gossip. 'I thought the Bird Lady a tragic woman, but she was doing alright.'

'Kirsty, forbidden love is always tragic. It would have been a very strained and tense relationship. No one gets what they really want.'

I decided not to push it any further…for now, but there were more juicy titbits to be had and I'd do some digging later.

Chapter Two

Sophie helped move Christopher and me to our new cell. I'd only been in there once before when we were being shown the priest hole. It was just as it had been, properly decorated and furnished, not an attic storage area as such, but even so, the worst room in the house. The skilling ceiling made it feel claustrophobic. I was surrounded by old brown furniture, not antique, just old, chipped and worm-holed, and standing on a tapestry rug half eaten by moths, probably more than a century ago.

When I got to the attic, I fiddled with the sash window to cool the room. It complained as I persuaded it to open but the wood was warped, and its paint peeled to the bone, so I could only get it half open. Then I took up position again by Christopher's side. The déjà vu was overwhelming; it was as if I hadn't moved in days.

Within the hour, however, his breathing eased. Could I escape for ten minutes to get a slice of toast and a cuppa?

My sister beat me to my act of agency and came to the door. 'Kirsty, go down and get something to eat. You need a break.'

'I'll be down in half an hour.'

'No, I've left Ottilie on her own, now is good.'

I stood up from the chair, my legs slow to take the new instruction.

On the way to the kitchen I passed Colin on the stairs. I don't like crossing on the stairs at the best of times. It's my only superstition, but it was also the first time I'd been alone with Colin for four years. Immediately, I remembered standing in the pub, talking about Colin as though he were a paedophile. The memory knocked me sideways: I could see it clearly now, I was out of line. I'd almost passed him, and the awkward moment would pass, but instead my shame propelled an outburst. 'I'm sorry, Colin,' I said, looking directly into his eyes, 'for the stupid things I said…in the pub.'

He stopped and smiled. 'I forgave you a long time ago. I'm sorry, I should have told you.'

That had me. My mouth was open, with nothing coming out.

'You're very welcome here, Kirsty. We've missed you.'

He reached out and patted me on the shoulder. It was fatherly, friendly, priestly. As if he were blessing me. Fortunately, he walked on, and I was released from having to respond.

I found Ottillie in the kitchen.

'Is Christopher okay now?'

'The same, just the same.' I said. I couldn't summon positivity.

'Aunty Kirsty, Christopher can play with me if he wants.'

'Sorry, Ottilie, he's just not well enough yet.'

Otillie was being a four-year-old, her world revolving around herself. She reminded me of myself at that age: into everything, everyone into her. Life had not had a chance to confound her yet.

Colin came into the kitchen.

Ottillie touched my hand and tried to find my eyes, 'Maybe, if I played with him, he'd get well?'

'Ottie,' Colin said, 'these things take time, be patient.'

I sat down in the chair by the Aga and put my head in my hands, taking a moment, feeling sorry for myself. I could have fallen asleep there and then, and only the presence of Colin and Ottilie kept me from floating off.

'I'm sorry I haven't been very present, Kirsty. I'm working on this Sunday's sermon: transmutation. I really need to avoid using the phrase "born again".' He chuckled. 'There are too many catch phrases that distract from the message.'

I felt Colin's hand on my shoulder and the clunk of a mug next to me. 'What would you like on your toast?'

'Just some spread, thanks.'

'Sophie and I have been praying for you and Christopher, and I would have asked the congregation to join us, but atlas, no congregation.' He chuckled again. 'I've managed, though, to get an online group set up. Just twenty of us or so, at the moment, but the word will spread. This Covid thing is a right menace.'

I remembered my conversation with Sophie, pleading with her that Christopher's fever wasn't Covid. In truth, how could I have known? They have been amazing taking me in. I cradled my mug and rested my eyes.

They had one of those station clocks and its ticking came into focus. I heard the Aga, creaking with the change of heat. The sounds of the kitchen were a welcome change from Christopher's snuffles. Then I smelt warm toast and butter, delicious, and it reminded me I was hungry.

Ottilie pushed her rag doll across the table. 'You can play if you want to, her name's Tabby.'

'Let Kirsty eat, Ottie, she's very tired.'

'I'm okay', I lied.

The door creaked and Sophie walked in. Her long black smock enveloped her breasts, hips and legs. She'd enjoyed flaunting her body at school, covering it with fashion and cosmetics and not much else. This vision of her as a chaste lady-of-the-house was, despite me seeing it for the last decade, still confusing, if not ridiculous.

'Christopher's doing okay,' Sophie said. 'I've put some new sheets on the chair. I'll give you a hand to change them.'

'You're both doing really well, darling,' Colin said. 'I'll make us something nice for supper later and you two can recover.'

Which two did he mean? Sophie and Christopher, or Sophie and me? I took Sophie's entrance as my cue to go back upstairs and grabbed my mug and toast.

Christopher was as I'd left him, sleeping. This was best for him, as sleep is restorative, but at some point I'd have to get some sustenance into him and maybe that would set off the fever again. I took up my usual position.

Last night he'd soaked the bed sheets with his sweat, and I'd spent hours on my phone, surfing the internet, looking for tips on how to cool him. Twice I'd called 111, first to see if someone would come out, and then to know at which point his temperature was critical. The symptoms were Covid-like, and that was enough for them to refuse sending someone.

I'd watched him turn red, watched my baby cry out in pain, and sigh as he gave in it to its torture. Sophie and I had run him a cold bath, not knowing if that was the right thing to do. At what point do you open the window and scream, 'Somebody help me, my son is dying'? Would anyone answer in a world full of people screaming out 'My loved one is dying'? Our world is dying from this plague. This global warming. This political madness before World War Three.

The hours passed, and in my sleeplessness, fear and anger filled my head with maddening negative thoughts: is there some arcane phrase I should say that would get the

NHS to respond? Did I turn off the central heating when I left home?

Sophie opened the door, no knock, no greeting. I feared my welcome was coming to an end. She must be as fed up as me. Together we changed the sheets. Then, without a word, Sophie gave the nod and I went to the kitchen for another brief reprieve.

Otillie was on her own, seemingly unmoved from the morning. It was dark outside, and a single candle burned on the table, flickering and illuminating the kitchen. It was one of those ivory church candles, about six inches tall and three inches in diameter. Only a low watt standard lamp in the corner assisted the lighting, making the kitchen quite dingy.

'Is Christopher ready to play yet?' Ottilie said.

'No, not yet. I don't know when.' If ever, I wondered. Probability felt like it was merging with impossibility. When? How much more could his small body take?

I looked around the kitchen. It had been attacked by some puritanical interior designer. There was no colour or design, not even a picture of Jesus performing miracles. The floorboards looked original, nearly a foot wide, and with centuries of filth between them. The window was covered by a simple grey blind. No T.V., pot plant or any of that blue and white crockery to cheer the place up. The only let up from the austerity was the deep blue of the Aga and a slogan above the mantel piece, hand painted in a cursive reddish-brown watercolour. It looked as if the writer had slit their wrist with their final thoughts and wrote using their own blood. "And by the power of the Holy Ghost, ye may know the truth of all things."

Unconsciously, I read it aloud.

'Holy Ghost?' Otillie repeated.

'It's what's written above the cooker.'

'Oh! Is that like Casper the Ghost? I've heard of him.'

At that point Colin walked in. Having to explain the Holy Trinity to a four-year-old no longer had to happen.

'No, Ottie, the Holy Ghost is very different,' Colin said, in his most enigmatic Reverend style.

'There's a ghost in the candle,' Ottilie said, looking at the candle on the table.

Thank God, this was an opportunity for some light-hearted chat. 'A candle ghost? That's sounds fun,' I laughed. 'What does a candle ghost do?'

Colin frowned: maybe my question was irreverent.

Ottilie spoke with an air of authority, no doubt absorbed from Colin. 'A candle ghost makes you unsick.'

Colin and I were silenced. Of all the things she could have said, something from Disney or Pixar, but no we got this: an offer of spiritual healing, something positive, something useful.

'I like that idea,' I said.

Ottilie frowned like Colin does, as if I'd demeaned her explanation.

'The candle ghost could unsick Christopher,' she declared.

'Ottie,' Colin said, 'come and get your pyjamas on and we'll make supper together.'

Colin was saved, as was I, from having to explain the difference between the Holy Ghost and a common or garden ghost. Part of me was disappointed and wondered what he would have said.

Back in the nursing room, I found Sophie kneeling in front of Christopher's bed, head bowed, hands together in prayer. She must have heard the door but didn't look up. 'The nighttime sweats have started,' she said, with little emotion. She left the room without looking at me.

This was bad. Could Christopher survive another night? Had he had enough water during the day to sweat any more out? This was a battle with dehydration. Had he eaten enough to replenish his body? This was a battle of survival. Christopher had not spent a moment of the day able to talk or even register my presence. He'd spent it trying to restore himself and now the long night threatened his existence. I sobbed silently, not wanting Sophie to hear. If only I was religious and could have found solace in prayer. Should I call 111 and give them an update? Should I browse the internet again to find the crucial tip I'd missed?

With my head in my hands all I could do was sob. But then a single memory came, of Ottilie telling me, "The Candle Ghost could unsick Christopher."

In less than a minute I was in the kitchen and fortunately found it empty. I grabbed the candle on its simple white ceramic dish and took it upstairs, placing it on Christopher's bedside table. The lip of the candle was lower on one side, and I turned it so that the flame shone over him.

I didn't feel foolish. I was doing everything I could. Out of the mouth of babes comes wisdom and as strange as a candle ghost might be, I wasn't taking any chances.

I turned off the bedside table and the candle came into its own. Pulling my chair closer, I rearranged the cushions for the long night ahead.

Suddenly there was a banging in the stairwell. Colin called up, 'Ottilie! Come out of the priest hole NOW.'

I waited for Ottilie to answer.

'OTTIE?'

'I'm not in there, Daddy, I promise.'

I ignored it. I had enough to worry about.

My eyelids were heavy, but I knew if I rested them I might fall asleep, and my attention wouldn't be on Christopher. I had to stay awake.

But I failed and was roused with more banging in the stairwell, this time louder. Maybe it just seemed that way because I was asleep. Then I heard someone call "MOTHER".

It wasn't Christopher, it had to be Ottilie.

Colin was remonstrating with Sophie, '…no, I'll do it.'

I heard his heavy footsteps come up the stairs, pause and then the priest hole door open. Its hinges complained from their infrequent use with a high-pitched whine, as if pleased to be released. Part of me was expecting to hear him challenge Ottillie again, but instead, he carried on up the stairwell.

'Kirsty? Are you decent?'

'Yes, come in.'

'Was Ottillie up here?'

'No, not recently.'

He looked disappointed, turned on his heel and left.

Then, slowly, the candle began to shine brighter. There must have been a new draught as I could hear it sizzle into life. The room was somehow more cozy and complete. Christopher's skin tone looked healthier, the shadows more subtle, less hostile. I had a new ally and its wick sat up proudly as if acknowledging my affection.

*

I must have dozed off, and it was the window closing that woke me. Sophie walked slowly from the window to Christopher's side. 'You borrowed the candle then?'

'Sorry, I just thought it more restful.'

'It's a bit dangerous having it so close to the bed.'

Sophie went to move the candle.

I put my hand on it. 'No, it's fine,' I said, managing not to sound too emotional. I kept my hand on the candle's plate until Sophie had taken a step back.

'Kirsty, Colin told me what Ottilie said.'

The room was cold, so it was good that Sophie had come to close the window. I put my hand on Christopher's forehead, which felt a little clammy but not too hot. I pushed the sheet away from his mouth. In my silence Sophie walked to the door.

'I'll bring some supper up,' she said, and then closed the door behind her.

The candle had burned down quite a bit. Its weeping rim was more pronounced, and a tear had appeared on one side with an ear of wax on one other.

Within the hour the room warmed up, maybe too warm, and I struggled to move the window half open again.

I didn't look at my phone or pace the room, I sat and watched Christopher breathe. The quiet of the room was only disturbed by the call of an owl and then, later, the ring of the church bell.

I was moving in and out of sleep. The ordeal of nonstop nursing had well and truly got the better of me, and I realised I'd been doing that unconscious drooping of the head and the automatic reflex of lifting it up again. I arched my back and straightened up to reduce the risk of deep sleep, but my eyes insisted on closing.

Chapter Three

It was Christopher's joyful giggle that woke me. His eyes were open and he was pointing, and I'd never seen him do that before. He was pointing to something in front of him, and his eyes told me it was close and engaging. But there was nothing I could see.

Then I realised what he thought was funny. The candle's dog ear had now developed into a jolly face. Two eyes, one open, one winking. Not a smile but a pout. The candle had slumped, and its sides had become cheeks. When I looked back at Christopher, he was asleep, as if he'd never been awake, as if I'd never seen him point, giggle or stare. Had I dreamt it?

I propped myself up again with the cushion under my elbow and straightened Christopher's bed clothes. He should have some water soon, but that would mean waking him.

I hadn't brought a bottle from home. I'd weaned Christopher off my breast when he was ten months and gone onto the bottle, and he'd been an early taker to the beaker. A beaker would be perfect now; maybe Sophie had one.

An eager draught blew from the window, reminding me it was open, and I looked up. Sitting on the ledge was an owl. I froze, because I'd never seen in an owl before. Not a wild one. It was mostly cream coloured, but it had a darker edge around its face, as if it were wearing a nun's habit. It had a brown pear-shaped head with a kind of hollowed face, as if someone had taken a couple of bites out of that pear. It wasn't looking at me, it was looking at Christopher.

We stayed like that for nearly half an hour. Initially, it was startling to see the bird, and if it had been a gull, a crow or a pigeon I think I would have scared it away. But it was somehow peaceful and comforting to have it there, as long as it stayed on the ledge of course. I wouldn't want it flying about.

My mind wandered. I thought of the Bird Lady's love for the priest. Maybe it was real love. After all, they both shared the same love for God. They were both Catholic. She'd had three years together with him, before her son died and two to three after. I wondered if he'd tried to help her with her loss. Of course he had, he must have been a rock for her.

The owl briefly bowed its head as if to get a better view of us. Then it did that weird thing and turned its head round to look out of the window.

She must have been a force of nature, to have brought the plundering sailor to heel and then chase him to England. And maybe she wasn't desperate at all and just fancied the priest. To be able to capture a pious man's heart was no mean feat. I think I had her all wrong. She'd loved life and was chasing her dreams.

But when her son died, she'd have wanted another. What did the priest want? As Sophie said, it was a forbidden love, and he would have been careful every time they made love. Every moment of that intense passion was a reminder of her loss, and that she could never have what she wanted. Making love opened a wound, a wound that could never heal.

Sophie came in, pushing the door with a tray. 'Sorry that took so long, but it's here now.' She set down a plate on the desk. 'Gosh, that candle's burnt down fast. It's supposed to be a forty-eight hour one. That'll be the draught from the window.' She walked to it, and I noticed the owl had gone.

'Can you leave it? I'd rather have the cool air.'

She didn't reply but instead turned to Christopher and felt his head. 'Better, I think,' she whispered. 'Try to eat something, Kirsty.'

'Do you have a beaker with a top? I thought it would be easier for Christopher.'

'Good point, I'll have a look.'

Sophie left and I reached out for Christopher's hand. It was hot, like a hot water bottle. I couldn't relax. That was the thing with the fever, it kept going and then coming back. Then I heard the flutter of wings and when I looked around the owl was sitting in the same position as before. It seemed transfixed, looking at Christopher, or was it looking at the candle?

The owl was tiny really, not much bigger than the span of a hand, and the flecks on its wings were beautiful. Some would say it was a little boring in its colouring, with only different shades of brown and cream, not the majesty of a peacock, but then nor did it have the peacock's vanity. The owl sat patiently, and, if anything, demurely. Why was it visiting me tonight?

Sophie again appeared around the door, 'here, this'll keep you stocked up.' She held a candle in her hand. 'I'll get this one changed over.'

'No!' Oops, that was a little loud. 'Just leave it there, I can change it, when the time comes,' I said, with greater equanimity.

Sophie placed it down, looking at me quizzically but did not protest. 'Come on, you've not touched your supper; you need the energy.'

'I'll have some, in a minute.'

23

'Are you sure you want the window open? It's quite cool now.'

We both looked at the window, its small Georgian panels reflecting the candle's light. The owl had gone again.

'Its fine, for now, but thank you.'

Sophie said nothing and left.

The new candle which Sophie had brought looked like an imposter next to mine, and I moved it over to the bookshelf. I pecked at my supper. I wasn't hungry, and the congealed gravy was a turn off. The potato, though cold, was all that I could manage.

I heard her before I saw her. Ottillie was giggling outside the door. She gingerly put her head around and then silently walked over to put her arms around me, while looking at Christopher. 'Maybe he can play tomorrow. The candle is helping.'

'He's still battling, I'm afraid.'

I looked at the candle. It had changed shape again, fatter in the belly and its 'eye' had closed so that it looked asleep.

'What happens when a candle ghost burns away completely?' I asked. I really did want to know.

'They go to heaven of course.'

'Of course.'

Ottillie looked towards my supper and then back at the candle. She was enjoying having me ask her for advice about the life of a candle ghost.

'The candle's almost gone,' Ottillie said. 'Let's thank him before he goes.'

'How do you know it's he, and not she?'

'It's a boy, you can tell.'

Ottillie was truly owning the space and it was lovely to see her so confident. It was a welcome distraction from my

24

exhaustion, and I needed everything I could to get me through.

'Oh, the bird is here too,' Ottillie said, pointing to the window.

'You've seen the owl before?'

'Is it an owl? It's not like the ones on CBeebies.'

'It's just a small one, that's all.'

'She's lovely.' Ottilie walked to the window and carefully knelt by the bird.

'And how do you know it's a she?'

'It's definitely a lady bird.' She held out her finger and the owl jumped onto it. I was speechless; this was amazing. The owl edged along Ottillie's finger and then nuzzled her beak along her hand.

'Mummy doesn't see the bird, but you do.'

'Yes, I do.'

'Christopher will be alright now. You can sleep with me in my bed, if you want.'

'That's very kind, but I'm just going to see it through till the morning. He'll start to cool down then. Thank you so much for telling me about the Candle Ghost.'

'That's okay. Night night, Aunty Kirsty.'

'Ottie, how did you know about the Candle Ghost?'

'Daddy told me, at church.' Ottilie fidgeted with her pyjamas. 'I asked why they light a candle and put it with all the others.

'But, why did you say about the unsick? That the candle would help?'

'Daddy said, as soon as they light the candle the pain starts to go away.'

I had no reply. Of course! I imagined Colin and Ottillie in the church, in front of all the votive candles that parishioners had lit in prayer. I hugged Ottilie tightly and she skipped away.

I was on my own again, and although Christopher was deeply asleep, it was still possible the fever would return fiercer than before. But I felt somewhere in my soul that it was, as Ottillie said, going to be alright, and I turned to the now very diminished candle, who seemed to be on his very last inch, with his mouth dribbling and his hair-knot-wick keeling over at a dramatic angle, a puddle of wax at his toes. 'Thank you candle, for all you have done, your light, your company and the hope you brought. I wish you peace in this life and the next.'

Suddenly the candle burst into life, as if I'd added gun powder. Its flame shot up ten times higher. A strange light consumed the room, shadows disappeared; everything was pierced by an electric white light. The candle hissed. It hadn't smoked before, but now a thick white plume rose to the ceiling, and like a mushroom it spread out from one side to the other before curling towards the floor.

'Mummy?' Christopher said softly. His eyes were opened wide, but he looked straight ahead, as if he were still asleep. The candle's huge flame reflected in his eyes. The smoke descended, enveloping us. Christopher stretched out his hand, pointing again.

'Christopher? Christopher are you awake?'

In an instant Christopher's arm fell back, his eyes closed and the candle went out. The room was pitch black.

I felt a downflow of air, heard the beating of wings and, very loud, an owl screech. It passed inches from me. I froze, frightened to the core. I hate being in the proximity of a flying bird. I thought it had landed, but when I got up, it screeched once more and passed so close, its wing went through my hair. Finally, I heard it land back on the window ledge and saw its silhouette.

I switched on the lamp and sensed a new void, a silence. The candle's fizzle had ended, the smoke had vanished.

I bent over Christopher, and he was gently breathing yet fast asleep. The candle had completely melted, with just a flat pool of wax covered by a thin opaque skin, trapping its wick.

I sat back in my chair and felt a rush of tiredness fall over me like a heavy blanket, and I had nothing to resist it. Within seconds I was asleep.

*

I awoke to calling: loud shouts of excitement. I could hear Colin and Sophie talking while running up the stairs. I looked for Christopher, but he was gone, his bed empty.

In the doorway Ottilie was standing with Christopher.

'Gosh, what a turnaround,' Colin said.

Sophie rushed forward and knelt in front of my chair, hugging me tight; Christopher joined the hug and then Ottillie, and finally, miraculously, Colin.

I was dizzy with elation and confused with lack of sleep, but I felt the squeeze of my family's hug and smiled for the first time in a week. I knew it wasn't the right moment, but I had to tell them my truth.

'Okay, you're going think this is crazy, but just before Christopher recovered last night, the candle kind of exploded into life. It let off all this smoke which gathered in a big mass around the ceiling, then it fell around us and a bird swooped in and screeched. It was the weirdest thing.'

I'd gabbled and now there was silence. I thought they'd mock me, that Colin would smirk, but no.

'Well,' Colin said, 'our Lord does move in mysterious

ways.'

Sophie kissed my cheek. 'I'm going to put the kettle on and make everyone some breakfast.

'I'll help,' Colin said.

'And me,' Ottillie said.

Once more, it was just Christopher and me.

'Mummy, I'm hungry.'

'Good, that's a very good sign.'

The sun now filled the room. There was a new peace, and the tingle of approaching joy; all was well. I felt an appreciation for the world. I'd been rescued by both known and unknown forces, by something beyond my control and I realised that I didn't need to know why or how, I could just be grateful.

Christopher was in front of me holding up Ottillie's rag doll. 'Look, Mummy.'

'That's Tabby, do you want one like it? Come on, let's get you changed into something clean for breakfast.'

I busied myself getting Christopher dressed. My neck was stiff, I was very tired, but my baby was most definitely unsick.

Christopher, as usual, wouldn't stand still as I put on his shirt. 'Mummy, where is the boy?'

'Which boy?'

'The boy in the night.'

'I think you mean Ottilie. She's making breakfast.'

Christopher looked confused but questioned me no further.

Suddenly I was frozen by an ear-piercing scream coming from downstairs, followed almost immediately by laughter. 'Sorry,' Sophie called up. 'I had a bit of a shock, everything's okay.'

Ottilie appeared, and in that unspoken agreement that

children have with each other, Christopher followed her out and downstairs, no doubt to play.

Sophie joined me soon after with a cup of tea.

'What was the scream?' I asked.

'Don't tell Ottillie,' she whispered, 'but I found a dead owl in the kitchen. I really don't know how it could have got there.'

'The owl I saw last night?'

'You saw an owl?' Sophie put her hand on my shoulder. 'Ottilie's always telling me about seeing a bird up here. It's a tiny thing, light brown?'

I nodded.

'Sorry I screamed but I just don't like things like that in the house and I thought it was only sleeping at first. It was on top of the Aga, just standing there, eyes closed. I only knew it was dead when I tried to push it out with the broom, and it just keeled over onto the floor. I really don't want to touch it.'

'I'll do it,' I said.

'Really?'

My poor wonderful owl, who'd been there for me. What a brief friendship. 'Do you have a shoe box, or something? I'd like to bury it. In the garden, if that's okay?'

Sophie didn't reply. She looked at me, at the window and then at Christopher's vacant cot. She smiled and nodded. 'You mean next to François' grave?' she whispered.

'The boy?'

'We know he's buried there now, from those church letters. It's the boy who died in the priest hole, but we don't like to tell people. People get freaked out by that kind of thing. Graves in gardens and not in graveyards. His grave is probably in Latin to hide his identity.'

'Why hide him?'

'Wrong creed, wrong nationality, unregistered and unloved. All he had was his mother and all she had was love from a man who wasn't allowed to love her.'

'What a start in life!'

'We don't know where Mademoiselle Oiseau is buried, although I strongly suspect she's with her son. Isn't that where the priest would have wanted her, nearby?

'Surely the graveyard.'

'I doubt they would have allowed it.'

'True,' I whispered, 'such hatred, such prejudice.'

Then Sophie gave me one of her lovely sisterly hugs. I welcomed it greedily and as she squeezed, I squeezed back. Looking over her shoulder I saw the remains of the candle and thought of his final goodbye to the world, and of the owl, so distraught, an echo of her screech shuddering through me. Or, perhaps, she too was saying goodbye and was in fact relieved to be there at his end. Who can say?

'I'm glad she had the love of the priest,' I said. 'It wasn't completely what she wanted, but it was love.'

'Who gets everything they want? Everything you need is a blessing.'

I looked at Christopher's empty cot. 'I'm so grateful I had you to call on.'

'And I'm so glad you did.'

Undying Love at the Trullo

Epigraph

A life of loving is not lost with death,
but the seed from which it draws its next breath.

L McEwen

Chapter One

Before leaving work, Kelvin had received a call from Bob, in which he learned that Bob's father had recently died.

Bob had been matter-of-fact; he was only calling to ask for Kelvin's opinion about the wording on a card. Bob wanted to write to his cousins to explain his father had died. Kelvin had never met Bob's father and remembering the picture of him Bob's grandparents had on their wall, could only vaguely recall him. There was no reason to be sad, yet there was no question about it, Kelvin was.

The thought of death and dying took hold of Kelvin, quietly and subtly transforming his drive home. Adding to this emotional vignette, the clocks had gone back an hour the day before, and now his commute was plunged into darkness. The lights of the oncoming cars glared through the light rain, as he studied the faces of their drivers and passengers, all of whom were unaware of his deepening mood: life was finite—we all die. But the usual addendum to this thought- life is short, better make the most of it- was lost on Kelvin. He was absorbed by the anger of being mortal, the tragedy that comes from loss.

He'd flicked on the radio for a distraction, but the radio presenter had been too upbeat and he quickly turned it off.

Just as Kelvin was pulling into his driveway, the skies had chosen that moment to drop their biggest downpour, and he'd had to make a run for his front door through the deluge.

He hurried inside and threw his keys in the bowl.

Helen, his wife, called from the kitchen. 'Hi, is that you? You alright?'

'No, we need to move, the commute is killing me.'

Helen appeared in the hallway and helped him take his coat off, which was rapidly making a puddle. She assessed Kelvin's mood.

'Hmm, okay, bad commute, but what else is wrong?'

Kelvin sighed. 'Bob's dad died.'

'Bob Turner? Oh! How is he taking it?'

'Okay, I guess, they weren't close. His dad lived in Italy.'

'Bob's Italian?' Helen said. 'But his surname is British.'

'Ah well, no, Bob's full name is Roberto Tornar.' Kelvin rolled the "r". 'He was born in southern Italy but spent most of his childhood in Bedford.'

'Where you were at school together?'

'Yeah! We'd go back to his house after school. He lived with his Grandparents. They were great, used to feed me delicious Italian grub. They came over in the fifties.'

Helen turned to go back to the kitchen. 'Why weren't Bob and his dad close?'

'His parents were caught up in their careers, either that or each other. They didn't make time for Bob and so it was decided he should live in England. Initially, Bob would go over on a visit, twice a year, summer and Christmas holidays, but when Giovanna, his mum, died, he and his dad completely lost touch.'

'When's the funeral?'

'That's long gone, he died about six weeks ago. Bob only found out yesterday, a letter from a solicitor. He's inherited his dad's house, and some outstanding loan. The solicitor wants him to settle the debt before they do the conveyancing of the house. It's only credit from the local grocery shop, so he's probably up overall.'

'Maybe, but some of those places aren't worth

anything. They have to nearly give them away. Did you see that show, *Italy's One Euro Homes*?'

'No, I think this one's okay, his dad was a carpenter.'

Helen poured them both a glass of wine. 'Hmm, he must be sad he missed the funeral.'

'Doubt it, he didn't go to his mum's.'

'You're joking! Who doesn't go to their mum's funeral?'

'You know Bob and his issues. I guess that's why he can be awkward—quiet.'

'They never bonded, so what! At some point you gotta get over it.'

'Hmm, okay, I know what you mean, but I've heard so many stories over the years. When his mum was home, her time was monopolised by Luigi, his dad. Bob would come back from school and they'd be in bed having noisy sex. Then they'd get up and have supper out, hardly saying hello to him.'

Helen passed Bob an onion and chopping board. 'He should go and check the property out.'

'That won't happen. Bob hasn't been to Italy in years. He hates that he can't speak the lingo.'

'Doesn't he want to bring his dad's stuff back home?'

'No!' Kelvin laughed. 'Helen, you just don't get it.'

'Where abouts in Italy was he?'

'Alberobello, Puglia. He had one of those cone-roofed houses.'

'A trullo?' Helen stood still and faced Kelvin. 'We should go.' She squeezed Bob's hand.

'Huh?'

'Yeah, it would be brilliant. Come on. You love Italy, and I think you could do with a cheer-up. Let's go and do Bob a favour and have a holiday at the same time. A few days in the sunshine.'

'And work? I can't just disappear like you can.'

'They'll be understanding. There's been a death.'

Kelvin laughed. 'We don't know if his house is liveable. We don't even know if there's hot water.'

'You said yourself he was a carpenter. It'll be liveable, and now since the funeral there's not even a dead body.'

'There's probably a dead cat and a load of mildew, and with those old houses, there's probably a hole in the roof, plaster falling off the walls and 1930s electricity and plumbing. You've probably got to use a well.'

'Come on love.' Helen wrapped her arms around Kelvin. 'Call Bob and sound him out.'

Kelvin sighed and picked up his phone. Bob answered.

'Hey Bob, like, Hel and I have been talking about your little problem and think we've got a solution.'

'About the inheritance?'

'Yeah. Look, first tell me about the state of this house. Is it together?'

'Oh yeah, well, Dad was good at that sort of thing.'

'He was a carpenter, right?'

'Yeah, but not furniture, more of a sculptor.'

'Wow, that's different. You never said.'

'Hmm, not my favourite subject.'

There was silence until Bob cleared his throat. 'Yeah, he could do all the house maintenance, but sculpture and whittling were his thing. He made quite a name for himself.'

'The house then, it's liveable?'

Bob laughed. 'Yeah, last time I was there he had it all sorted. Up to date kitchen and bathroom. A groovy outside terrace, actually.'

'Hel and I thought we'd go over for you. Check out the

house and take a load of pictures. You could decide what you wanted to do with the place.'

'Really, you're sure? That would be great.'

'We love Italy, so yeah, no problem.'

'Kelvin, I'd really appreciate that. I've been thinking about it and, yeah, I just couldn't face it. I haven't been back since Mum went. That's got to be over nine years now.'

'Did he ever think of remarrying?'

'No, he told me no one could replace her. Well, I'm paraphrasing, he actually swore at me for suggesting it.'

'It's unusual to want to remain single…for a bloke anyway. I guess he was still in love?'

'They were infatuated, early nights, romantic dinners. Dad would write her poetry, sing to her while she was in the bath. I felt like a gooseberry.'

'Jesus!'

'Oh yeah, they were in love. Well, Dad was in lust anyway. I always wondered what Mum thought of all the attention. She didn't get much time off.'

'Can you send us a pic of the place, on your phone?'

'Sure, doing it now.'

'Is it actually in the town? Can we get there by taxi?'

'Yeah, in the old town, so the last twenty metres you have to walk. All the buildings are like over six hundred years old. After landing in Bari, you'll be in Alberobello within the hour.'

'What a cool name.'

'It means beautiful tree.'

A photo appeared on Kelvin's phone and Helen pulled it towards her to see.

It was of a five coned trullo, beautifully restored, with flowers in hanging baskets and an olive tree shading a terrace. Helen put her cheek against Kelvin's and ran her hands through his hair. She beamed at him and kissed his lips.

Kelvin chuckled as he tried to get his phone back to his ear. 'Bob, I think we're definitely up for it. When can we go?'

Helen was pulling on Kelvin's shirt and mouthing, "Now, now, now".

'Whenever you want, it's not like there's anyone there.'

'Cool, right! We'll make our excuses at work and go check it out.'

'You'll need a key,' Bob said. 'I'll pop it round tomorrow.'

*

The next afternoon Helen was at home on a video call with her boss and had brought the subject around to the timing of holidays. Her boss confirmed that they weren't particularly busy at that moment and so Helen pounced on the opportunity to ask for the following week off.

Within minutes of obtaining her freedom there was a knock at the door. Still euphoric, she opened the door with gusto.

'Bob!'

'Hi, sorry, I did text, is this a bad time?'

'No, I'm sorry, it's been a busy afternoon.'

'I brought the key, that's all.' Bob said, while looking behind Helen.

It was awkward, and Helen realised she hadn't been on her own with Bob before. 'I'm really sorry to hear about your dad.'

Bob looked non-plussed. 'Okay, so the key.' He

fumbled in his coat pocket and finally held it up.

'Wow, that's some key.'

Helen took it and Bob remained standing there, not saying anything.

'Would you like a cuppa?' Helen offered.

'Yeah, great, thanks.'

As they walked to the kitchen Helen examined the key. It was heavy, yet ornate, about six inches long, and on the head of the key was the face of a crowned man. On one side he was smiling and on the other frowning.

Helen flicked on the kettle. 'Do you want anything from the house? We could bring back quite a bit, we'd just have to pay for extra luggage.'

'Hmm, no I don't really want anything. I think the solicitor will be clearing it out.' Bob stepped up onto the bar stool, looking uneasy. 'There is one thing, I guess. My father made a mask for me when I was eighteen. People said it was the spitting image of me. Luigi, that's my dad, was a master painter as well as carver. When I put the mask on it didn't look like I was wearing a mask, it was like me being me. But it was fun wearing it. People were really freaked out by it.'

'What was it for then?'

'Dad wanted to hang it on the wall, you know, like having a picture of me.'

'Not really a present for you then?'

Bob shifted uneasily on his feet. 'It'll be above the front door. It was one of the few things Dad did to celebrate me.'

'Kelvin told me you had a rough childhood.'

'Oh, you know, I don't like to complain.' Helen left a silence for Bob to fill and carried on making the tea.

'In their prime, they were a famous couple.'

'How famous?'

'Giovanna, my mum, met the Pope and dad has a sculpture in the Peggy Guggenheim Museum in Venice.' Bob sighed, 'They just weren't very good at getting old, probably tried to hold onto youth for too long. Dad even tried to flirt with the sister of one of my girlfriends.'

'What!'

'Yeah, it was bit weird, she was only like fifteen, when he was mid-fifties or something.'

'I thought he was besotted with Giovanna.'

'Oh, yeah, that was his big love, but I'm talking about sex. When Mum was on tour he just didn't want to miss out. Then Mum went the same way. One time when she was in London, there were reports in the papers of her having an affair. She returned home and then two weeks later the man was found dead. It was an apparent suicide, you know, because she'd left him. But in Alberobello, they knew Dad had disappeared for nearly a week and suspected he'd got his revenge. That's what they were saying in the bars anyway.'

'Hmm, yeah, that does sound like a pretty intense relationship. That must have shaken you up.'

Helen wondered if that accounted for Bob's shyness, his lack of confidence. When you're young you want to know the world is dependable, predictable and that at least your parents think your special.

Chapter Two

The flight had been fun. They'd had advance warning about the budget airline and geared up for its shortcomings with a picnic, a laptop for Kelvin and a Kindle for Helen.

Outside Bari airport, Kelvin dashed to the nearest taxi, but the driver kept his window down and pointed to the front of the queue of taxis. Kelvin dragged their luggage to the first taxi in the line, leaving Helen to catch up. Before he could knock on the driver's window, the driver stepped out.

Kelvin had prepared himself. 'Buongiorno, voglio andare Alberobello adesso. Quanta costa per favore?'

The taxi driver smiled and answered in fluent, flowing Italian. Kelvin was waiting for a number and wasn't sure if the taxi driver had said one, so he repeated his pre-planned sentence. The taxi driver smiled again, brought out a packet of cigarettes and wrote a number on the cover.

'Va bene, grazie,' Kelvin said.

'Okay.' The driver placed their luggage in the boot and Kelvin was invited to sit in the front.

Within ten minutes they were out of the airport complex, on a dual carriageway, competing with the other traffic. The sun was shining, the Italian countryside was resplendent, and soon they were passing acres of vineyards for as far as the eye could see.

Helen pointed, 'Look, there's a sign for Monopoli.'

'Wait, there's an actual place called monopoly?'

They had a good giggle. The driver said something in Italian and Kelvin nodded enthusiastically, so the driver spoke some more. Kelvin wasn't too sure what he'd said, but it was nice to hear Italian spoken.

When they were about half an hour from Alberobello they saw their first trullo. 'Look, there's one,' Helen said. The structure had the quaintness of a hobbit house and although it suited the landscape, it was clearly born of a different era. The beautiful conical shape of the roof with its ornate pinnacle and whitewashed symbol was captivating.

'They're gorgeous, aren't they?' Helen said. 'Do you think Bob's will be like that?'

'I think so, but Bob's has got five cones. I read they were designed to be dismantled when the tax inspector called. They'd literally pile up the stones onto some carts and drive them away.'

'They look a bit heavy for that. I heard it was because of the warring factions in the region. Sometimes they had to leave the area in a hurry, but at least they could take their houses with them.'

As they approached Alberobello, the number of trullo houses increased and either Helen or Kelvin would call out enthusiastically, 'There's one!' The driver could not hide his amusement. Very soon they pulled into the centre of Alberobello and were surrounded by hundreds.

'Wow, look at all these trullo,' Kelvin said.

'Trulli,' the driver corrected. 'Plural is trulli. Okay? You will find fifteen hundred trulli in Alberobello. I think you guys are going to love it here,' he said in near perfect English.

Helen and Kelvin looked at each other. Their driver had been withholding the degree of his linguistic competence.

The sun was beginning to set, and when the car turned down the narrowest of lanes, spread out before them, bathed in rose tinted sunlight, was a beautiful hillside covered in trulli. The lane became so narrow the driver had to contract his wing mirrors to get past a parked car. They carried on up a steep hill to a tiny turning circle surrounded with beautiful rustic homes.

'You have to make forty metres walking,' the driver said.

'We can cope with that.' Helen laughed.

The taxi driver went to the boot and pulled out their luggage.

Helen took out her ornate key.

'Ah, okay! You don't have an AirBnb then?' the taxi driver said, looking at the key.

'No, it's our friend's house, he's just inherited it.'

'Da chi…from who?'

'Luigi Tornar.'

The driver froze. 'Luigi and Giovanna Tornar?'

'Yeah, well Giovanna died a while back…' Kelvin started to explain.

But the tax driver wasn't listening. He made the sign of the cross and grabbed the money, Kelvin had held ready. Without a word he got into the car and sped off, tyres screeching.

'That was weird,' Helen said.

'Hmm, or rude. Come on, let's find our holiday home.'

Helen followed Kelvin up the path lined with trulli, each dragging their luggage behind them. Up close the structures seemed smaller. They all appeared to be a single storey, and only a quarter of them showed signs of life. The path climbed gently and twisted around to a confluence of three separate routes.

Kelvin counted out the door numbers aloud, '…number eight. Here we go, number nine.'

They stopped outside a long house.

'Yup, that's it,' Helen said. 'There's the five cones.'

Kelvin approached the door and tentatively knocked. 'You never know, we don't want to walk in on someone.'

Their knocking attracted the attention of the neighbours, and an old man in his eighties opened his door.

'Buongiorno,' Kelvin said.

'Buonasera,' Helen corrected.

The man was silent and closed the door loudly.

'That's rude,' Helen said. 'Come on, let's go in.'

Kelvin took the key from Helen. The lock needed some persuasion. It took nearly a minute to find the correct sequence of pulling, pushing and turning. Finally, it creaked open.

Helen found the light switch and to the surprise of both of them, the lights came on, illuminating a modern but small kitchen. It could only have been ten feet square.

'What's that smell?' Helen asked.

'Smells like ripe fruit to me. Better than damp and mould though.'

'Come on, let's explore.'

They walked from the kitchen into the living room, furnished with a sofa and dining table. The walls were lined with wooden ornaments and ceramics. A wooden rocking chair stood patiently in one corner and a floor standing sculpture of a horse, rearing on its hind legs, filled another.

'Wow, I didn't realise all his possessions were going to be here. It's like he's still at home.'

'Come on, what's next?'

There were two doors to choose from, and Helen led the way to the one behind the sofa. They found a bedroom containing a double bed with wardrobe, two bedside tables and a valet stand, with Luigi's jacket and trousers still on it, and his black shoes underneath.

'Ugh, no T.V.'

'We'll make our own entertainment,' Kelvin said, pinching Helen's bottom.

Helen walked through to the next room, discovering a bathroom, which again was the same size as all the other rooms.

'No bath then,' Helen said, with disappointment.

'I guess they didn't have the water to fill it back then.'

'What, from the well you mean?' Helen chuckled.

Helen walked back to the living room and opened the other door facing the sofa. It revealed another bedroom, fractionally smaller, but with a double bed, nonetheless. There was again the same large assortment of wooden sculptures on the wall: masks, horses, turned pots, arranged flowers, puppets.

'What's through there?' Kelvin said, pointing to a door on the other side of the bed.

Helen opened it. 'Hmm, nothing much, it's only a storage area.'

Long shelves of pots, tools and suitcases, lined the walls. On the top shelf were bottles of pickled vegetables, olives and fruits.

'We'll have the first bedroom then, with the ensuite,' Kelvin said. 'This must be the guest bedroom.'

'As long as you move Luigi's suit in here.'

Kelvin chuckled, 'Come on, let's leave the unpacking and go find a restaurant.'

'Shall we have Italian or Italian?'

'I think I'd prefer an Italian tonight.'

They opened the front door and found two old couples talking quietly, with heads bowed together, yards from the door.

'Buongiorno,' Kelvin said.

'Buonasera,' Helen corrected.

The two couples fell silent, turned to each other and then walked off. But they didn't go far, one couple retreating to number ten and the other to number seven.

'That's rude,' Helen said.

'Maybe it was my accent.'

Half an hour later they were in the town centre, sitting at a restaurant with an English menu, sipping Aperol Spritz. By ten o'clock they were the last to leave. It was more of a stagger than a walk home, but joyful, nonetheless.

This time it was Helen who opened the door, and it opened straight away.

'I must have loosened it,' Kelvin said. 'Shall we have a nightcap?'

'I've had enough, but maybe there's some herbal tea.'

Kelvin went into the living room to search for a drinks cabinet. Helen explored the kitchen cupboards. Five minutes later they sat around the kitchen table, Helen sipping something she didn't quite recognise, but which was definitely herbal, and Kelvin sipping something clear and definitely alcoholic. The taste reminded him of something between cheap brandy and disinfectant.

'It's probably grappa,' Helen said.

'Don't know, the label was in foreign.'

On the table was a tall white ceramic vessel with a wide cap. Its lid was dark wood and highly polished. Next to it sat a wreath of brown flowers and dried greenery.

'Unusual vase,' Kelvin said.

'Hmm, probably not a vase.'

'What then?'

'An urn.'

'Urn?'

'As in ashes.'

'Ashes?'

'Kelvin! It's probably Luigi's ashes.'

'Oh! Why do you say that?'

'Because Luigi's dead and was cremated, and there was no one around to receive his remains.'

'Oh! Do we want him on the kitchen table?'

'No, we should move it.'

'Okay, where are you going to put him?'

Helen tutted. 'I'll put it in that storeroom,' she picked up the urn.

'May as well take the wreath too.'

'I think we can throw that; those funeral flowers are definitely over.'

'Brown bread?'

'As a dodo.'

Helen picked up the wreath. 'There's a copy of the order of service here too.'

'Read it to me at bedtime, I like it when you talk Italian.'

'Kelvin, that is very wrong.'

Helen took the urn away while Kelvin studied the kitchen more thoroughly. On the wall and mantelpiece were old photos and newspaper clippings celebrating Luigi's career. One of the framed articles showed an aerial view of hundreds of people filling the road to their trullo.

'Hey, look at this, Helen. The man was quite famous. I mean, Bob said he was, but this is really impressive. Looks like he had quite a few national exhibitions, and there's an article that talks about a show in Milan.'

'Wow, you're Italian has really come on,' Helen teased.

'Okay, I saw the word Milan and Exbo, you don't have to be a genius.'

Helen yawned, 'Right, are you taking me to bed?'

'Well Luigi isn't.'

'Oh, God, don't.'

Helen followed Kelvin to the bedroom, and Kelvin flicked on the lights. 'What's that!' On the double bed were two sets of clothes, neatly folded, one on each side of the bed.

Helen looked horrified, 'It looks like they're all set to get dressed in the morning.'

Kelvin lifted the black trousers. 'I think this might have been his funeral garb.'

Helen unravelled her pile and held up a long black dress. 'Snap! But she died, like, ten years ago?'

'Yeah, and anyway, you don't dress for your own funeral.'

'This is creepy, I'm taking these out.' Helen picked up the two piles and took them to the guest room.

Kelvin's phone rang.

'Bob?'

'How is it?'

'Yeah, nice place. You should keep it as a holiday home.'

'Nah. Weird memories.'

'Talking about weird, this neighbourhood's a little unfriendly. We tried to say hello and they couldn't get away fast enough. I thought your dad was a local celebrity.'

'He was until mum died. After the funeral people thought he'd find another signorina. A lot of the local ladies were peeved when he spurned their advances. They couldn't understand why he wasn't interested when he was clearly such a romantic, and that's putting it politely. They didn't like how he kept on about mum. Some said he'd

47

gone mad, acting as if she was still alive, not having anyone talk about her as if she were dead. He went from local celebrity to local crackpot.'

'Proper loco.'

'He'd have conversations with himself, as though she were there, even shouting matches, but he was, like, doing both parts. The neighbours swore they could hear them making love.'

'Yes, that's most definitely unhinged.'

'They lived out their whole lives as if it were an opera, always some great drama going down. Their breakups and reconciliations were legendary. Giovanna once destroyed one of his sculptures on display at the town hall. Luigi had to make another to replace it.'

'Hmm, by the way, are you sure you don't want anything? There's a lot of cool stuff here. It's probably worth something.'

'The solicitors will get an agent in to deal with all of that. Maybe that's proved too difficult with Dad's reputation. Some of the locals are terrified and won't go near the place.'

Bob and Kelvin chatted some more and when Kelvin rang off, Helen started.

'They might find it too difficult to sell this place. We could get it cheap.'

'What would we do with it?'

'You could improve your Italian for a start, and we could rent it out when we're not here.'

'Did you hear the part about it being scary and Bob having weird memories about it?'

'They're his memories and I don't scare easily.'

Once in bed Helen remembered her conversation with Bob. 'Kevlin, Bob mentioned one thing. He wants his mask, the one Luigi carved of him. It should be above the kitchen door.'

Kelvin immediately got up and looked above the kitchen door, but there was just a wooden carving of a man and woman kissing. On closer examination, he noticed it appeared a little more lewd. The limbs of the couple were chaotically entwined in rapture with a plant of some kind, and the man seemed to have a rather long member, badly disguised as part of the plant's trunk. 'Nothing like Bob's face here,' he called to Helen.

'Maybe, it's outside, he was pretty definite.'

Kelvin opened the door and looked up. There was a carved face, but it looked nothing like Bob.

Kevlin got back into bed, 'I guess after nine years, Luigi gave up and took it down. He knew Bob wasn't coming back.

*

Having slept for a few hours, Bob found himself wide awake at 3am. His head was filled with the artistic ambience of the trullo and the notoriety of the couple whose home it had been. He crept out of bed and went exploring.

In the living room he turned on the standard lamp. Its column was beautifully carved, as if a vine had grown up and around it, forming at the top a pedestal seating a cupid with bow and arrow. The grappa bottle was on the dining table, and he refilled his glass. Sitting on the sofa, he examined the room more closely. Luigi had been very prolific with his wood carving. It was extravagant, elaborate and intricate. Not to everyone's taste by any means, it was a style you either hated or loved. Kelvin decided he loved it.

Then he realised the nest of tables was carved too. A snake twisted up one leg, trying to eat its own tail. A scene was carved into the table's surface, of a village setting of trullo houses. It was probably Alberobello itself. He'd used the wood grain to emphasise the cone of each trullo. There were people going about their daily business: a market stall holder selling his produce, a dog chasing a cat, a shepherd driving his flock down a lane. It was an ingenious design.

Kelvin sat back and gazed at the walls. There wasn't much blank space left, its surface was so crammed with Luigi's work. But it wasn't overbearing, and the pieces seemed to work together.

If Luigi's studio was at home, why hadn't they come across it? Kelvin drained his glass and stood up. What had Helen and he missed on their self-guided tour? Perhaps he'd rented a place nearby. No that didn't compute: Bob had definitely said his dad had worked from home.

Kelvin noticed something out of place on the wall: a long piece of wood, eighteen inches long, rounded at one end into a small ball shape, while the other end was bulbous like a small onion. Above a wooden plaque was another piece with the same shape. They were deeply polished, and Kelvin ran an appreciative finger along one. They were warm, beautifully carved, but what were they?

Then his eye fell on two ceramic pots, decorated with blue flowers on a white background, which were sitting on a cradle of wood. The cradle was rounded at the back into what resembled a giant butterfly shape, coming down into two small loops. Surely it was a pelvis. Kelvin placed the pots on the floor and removed the wooden pelvis from the wall. It wasn't strictly skeletal, or anatomical. It was as if a child had caught the essence of a body with a brush and then whittled away to make something beautiful. Kelvin rubbed its surfaces, admiring the wonderful curve of the arches, and then found something different at the back, a groove with straight sides. What was that for?

Kelvin pondered and decided refilling his glass would help. It only took one sip to make the connection. He reached up to one of the long, round-ended pieces and took it off the wall. Offering it up to the pelvis, it snapped into place: it was made to measure. Kelvin slotted in the other leg and then wiggled them around. They moved just like legs should, they wouldn't rotate extremely to one side and neither did they fall out when he held just the pelvis.

'Luigi, what were you up to?'

Kelvin took another swig and sat down on the sofa, looking intently at the wall. Within five minutes he had located all the other body parts. He got to work, bringing them down off the wall and covering the sofa and coffee table with them. In half an hour he'd built a man. It wasn't an ugly skeleton. It was elegant, curvaceous. It wouldn't do as an anatomical model to teach doctors. No, this was different, the rib cage didn't have each rib separated, its form was of a chest with pecs. The hands were objects of beauty in their own right.

But there was one small and slightly creepy problem: Kelvin couldn't find the head. He opened the cupboard doors, and even searched the storeroom, but no face. There was, however, a slot at the top of the spine to connect it. He almost wanted to wake up Helen; she was good at finding things.

Still, Kelvin marvelled at this life scale model and sat it on the sofa next to him. He wasn't a tall man, about three inches shorter than Kelvin.

'Do you want a drink mate?' Kelvin lifted his glass to

his new creation. 'If you don't mind, I'm going to call you Luigi, but if that doesn't suit, just shout.'

He decided the best thing to do was to put Luigi on the guestroom bed. He imagined Helen getting up and making them coffee in the morning and then seeing Luigi on the sofa; that wasn't fair on her. He laid the skeleton down and then realised he'd left the storeroom light on.

As he stepped through, to turn it off, he noticed a darker grout around some of the floor tiles. It was in a rectangular shape about a yard square.

'Hello, what's this then?'

He hunted and soon found what he was hoping for, a ring- pull to lift the floor hatch. It came up easily and the hinges allowed it to lean back against the wall, revealing a spiral of stone steps. Kelvin used the torch on his phone to follow them. Within seconds his nose told him he'd found the studio, as the smell of cut wood, turpentine and linseed oil filled his nostrils. Then he found the light switch and confirmed it. This was Luigi's studio.

The stone staircase opened out into a cellar with a barrel ceiling, about seven feet in height, but very long and quite wide, indeed it must have run the entire length of the building. There were piles of wood, off-cuts, rough timber, planed wood and even a tree trunk. A long workbench was piled high with work-in-progress. Luigi had obviously been working up until the day he died. At the end was an ancient lathe, a small kiln and other equipment he didn't recognise.

The walls were lined with shelves. There were hundreds of tins of paint, dyes and bottles of screws, nails and other fixings. There were piles of chisels, saws, hammers and other carpentry paraphernalia. Then he noticed a small window. It was pitch black outside and the pane only reflected the bare light bulb. Underneath was an old gramophone, the wind-up kind, with a record waiting to be played.

'Luigi, what a studio. You knew how to treat yourself.' Kelvin was consumed with cellar envy.

He picked up a chisel and felt its point. It was freshly sharpened, and the wooden handle had a wonderful feel; Luigi's hand had no doubt worked it smooth over the decades. He picked up a paint brush still resting in a dish of dye and let it drip back into the dish. It was as if Luigi were here yesterday.

Further along the workbench, Luigi's latest project was still in the vice, although partially covered with a white cloth. A   clamp held another piece of wood to it, maybe holding it as some glue dried.

'Hmm, what were you making Luigi?' Kelvin lifted the white cloth and revealed a mask, unpainted, and a little rough to the touch.

Briefly, he contemplated waking Helen to show her his find. Or should he go to bed so that he could enjoy the studio and further explorations of it in the morning? Instead, he skipped upstairs and fetched the grappa. As he passed Luigi's urn in the storeroom, he patted it. 'Well done old boy, you knew how to live.'

He came back down the spiral steps and put the record on. It was Italian opera, a woman singing soprano, and it was exquisite. Kelvin filled his glass and sat on the stool. 'I could get used to this.'

Kelvin compared his days at the office to Luigi's days in the studio, in his exhibition spaces, days wining-and-dining Giovanna. Kelvin had an opportunity here. Helen had suggested buying the place. Could he be happy in Alberobello? Kiss the commute goodbye, the stressful deadlines, the passive aggressive juniors, the overbearing directors?

Kelvin picked up a paint brush and tested its colour on an offcut. It was a rich dark red, like a ruby port. He twisted the lid of another bottle of dye and poured a little into a small dish. Again, he tested it, and this time he found a yellow tint, like a field of wheat. This was fun. Then he noticed a section on the shelf dedicated to sandpaper. All the grades were there.

Kelvin took a swig of grappa and tasted its earthiness, its force of nature and the complexity of its flavour. It was the taste of Italy and it warmed him and his imagination.

'Come on then Luigi, show me how it's done.'

Kelvin unwound the vice and took out the mask.

'How hard can it be?'

Chapter Three

It was the sound of a dog barking that woke Helen. She reached out for Kelvin with her foot but found a cold patch instead. Her phone showed her it was nearly one. She'd properly overslept.

The relaxing component of the holiday came into focus. It was cosy in bed and the idea of getting up unappealing. She lay and listened to the sounds of the house and heard talking outside. It sounded like Kelvin, but who was he talking to?

Helen decided to investigate. She quickly dressed and opened the front door. Sure enough, Kelvin was talking with a couple. There was something not quite right, something strange. Then through her sleep fug she realised what it was: Kelvin was talking Italian.

Kelvin saw her and waved, holding up a red and silver packet, then a brown bag.

He's jolly, Helen thought, and when has he ever waved like that?

The couple waved to her too, 'Buongiorno.'

'Buongiorno,' she returned, grateful they'd finally found a friendly local.

The couple made their goodbyes and Kelvin walked back to Helen, stopping to kiss her. 'Hi, you slept well.'

'Yes, couldn't you sleep?'

'Time's all out of sync, isn't it? We're like an hour ahead. I've got coffee and pastries, so breakfast is covered.'

'I'm famished, can't we go and find a restaurant?'

'Yeah, yeah, right after breakfast.'

Helen frowned but followed Kelvin inside. He grabbed

the moka coffee pot off the hob and started to fill it from the tap.

'Kelvin, when did you learn to speak Italian?'

'Oh, you know, I wasn't really speaking it. Just odd words thrown together. You wave your hands around and people know what you mean.'

'What were you talking about?'

'They told me how they bought a trullo in the next village along, their weekend house. They usually work in Bari, at the ferry terminal. They come here to get away. They've got a couple of kids that visit them. He's a financial controller and she does marketing for Superfast Ferries.'

'And this was all in Italian?'

'Yup, no big deal.'

Kelvin unpacked the pastries onto a plate and got the espresso cups ready.

'Wow, what's this?' Helen picked up a mask from the kitchen table.

'Something I was making, well, painting, last night.'

'It's of Luigi, isn't it?'

'Uh?'

Helen pointed to one of the photographs on the wall, of Luigi receiving a prize. She held up the mask next to it. 'It's him!'

'Er yeah, I guess. That's a bit strange though.'

'Why?'

'Because I just painted it, not from a photo.'

'So now you're not only talking Italian but you're a master painter?'

'We could do with some sugar. Do you want to look in that storeroom?'

'Change the subject, why don't you?'

Helen walked off leaving Kelvin holding the mask, peering into Luigi's eyes. He heard the coffee start to boil and took it off the heat. Suddenly there was a scream.

'Helen?'

Kelvin rushed to the guest bedroom to find Helen crouched down at the end of the bed.

'What's up?'

Helen could only point. She was pointing at the dressed skeleton on the bed.

'Oh God, sorry Helen, I should have said.'

'What do you mean, you should have said?'

Helen was horrified.

Kelvin explained about finding the interconnecting pieces, about dressing the skeleton so that it was less scary, about deciding to call him Luigi, about finding the studio and staying up all the night painting. Helen examined the skeleton.

'What do you mean, interconnecting pieces?'

'It's a bit like Lego, except this is off the scale craftmanship.' Kelvin pulled back Luigi's sleeve and disconnected the hand from the arm, then snapped it back together.

Helen took a step closer. 'Wow, wait a minute.'

Helen walked off leaving Kelvin with Luigi. He sat the figure up against the pillow. Somehow it seemed demeaning to leave him there prostrate while talking about him.

Helen came back holding the mask from the kitchen. 'Try this for size.'

'Yeah, if it is Luigi, I'd better put it on Luigi.'

Kelvin offered up the mask and sure enough it snapped on. 'Made to measure. Look at the attention to detail. It is truly amazing. The way the grain runs together when the

57

joints are slotted. He must have taken ages searching for the right piece of wood, taking advantage of its natural bend and twist. He was really devoted to his work, and he must have been consumed by how amazingly intricated human beings are. The wonder of existence.'

'Okay, so now you've turned into an art critic too.'

'I've been thinking about it, that's all. I was up all night.'

'But how did you find all these pieces? Where were they?'

'They were just hanging on the wall, just scattered amongst all the knickknacks and sculptures. I guess because there were so many pieces, it was difficult to make out, when we first arrived. Look, there's probably more here.' Kelvin pointed to the bedroom wall. 'Yeah, look, there's another pelvis.'

Helen studied the wall. 'And here's a leg. I tell you what, I've seen another mask as well.' Helen pointed through the door to a mask taking central position above the dining table. 'It's a similar size to Luigi's, but it's a woman.'

'I'll show you how easily it all goes together.' Kelvin fetched the pelvis from the wall. Again, it was holding two ceramic bowls. He offered up the leg. 'See, it just snaps into place. The accuracy is incredible. Wait till I show you his studio. He must have lived half his life down there.'

Helen held the pelvis and leg in awe.

Kelvin took the pelvis back. 'I tell you what, you put this one together if you want, I shouldn't have all the fun.' He chuckled. 'Right, I'm going to pour the coffee.'

He went through to the kitchen and busied himself making the table presentable.

'Hey Helen,' he called out, 'don't worry about the

sugar, it was hidden in pot labelled zucchero.'

He found his half-drunk bottle of grappa on the worktop and hid it away in a cupboard. The coffee pot only made enough for a shot glass of coffee each and so he put on another batch. 'Alright, Helen, breakfast is served,' he called.

Helen came through to the kitchen a little pensively and sat down. 'I might just skip breakfast, lunch is calling.'

'Look at these babies though, this one is pistachio, and this is marmalade. Apparently, they make them in the middle of the night, like 4 am. His name is Marco, the baker. And his family has been running the bakery for the last forty years.'

'And he told you this in English?'

'No, he doesn't speak a word of English, but you know how you muddle through.'

'Last night you didn't get a word that the taxi driver said, nor the waiter.'

'It takes time to tune your ear in, doesn't it?'

Helen picked up the funeral service leaflet. 'Can you read this?'

'No, I can't read a word, you know that.'

Helen skimmed the leaflet while sipping her espresso. 'Hmm, there's a hyperlink on here, I think we can see a video recording of the service.'

'Great, can't wait.' Kelvin chuckled.

'No, come on, we should watch it.' Helen got her phone and tapped in the hyperlink. 'Here you go, we might need to send this to Bob.' Helen pressed play.

The camera was a static one. The video had been recorded from the rear right side of the crematorium, showing twenty or so empty rows of seats, the coffin at the front and a priest or celebrant next to it. Three large bouquets of flowers were displayed next to the coffin. The priest started talking, addressing an empty auditorium.

'Why is he bothering?' Kelvin said. 'There's no-one there.'

'I guess he's addressing the video camera. Since Covid a lot of people are watching funerals on video, rather than attending.'

'Ooh, who's that?'

A woman in black appeared in the back row, moving along the line of seats, and sat down. Her dress was full length, with long sleeves, and she wore gloves. Her face was turned away from the camera, but from the side you could see she wore a veil. The priest started to sing in what Kelvin and Helen guessed was either Italian or Latin. It was something that not even Kelvin could understand.

'Do you want to finish this? I mean, it's a bit boring,' Kelvin said.

'Don't you want to know who that woman is? Bob said Luigi never got a new girlfriend after Giovanna died.'

The woman turned to the camera. Through the veil they could see her face was deathly white.

'Bob said his dad had never contemplated moving on,' Helen continued, 'Giovanna was the only woman he ever wanted.'

At that point the woman nodded to the camera.

Helen pressed stop. 'That face. I know that face.'

Kelvin was tucking into his pastry. 'Helen, come on, finish your breakfast first.'

But Helen had gone back to the living room. 'Kelvin! Come here.'

'Oh God, really?' Kelvin whispered. 'Can't I sit and just enjoy this pastry?'

'Kelvin!'

Kelvin went through to the living room. Helen was standing in front of the table staring at the wall.

'Look.'

'Look at what?'

'It's her, the mask, it's the woman from the funeral.'

'Kind of, yeah,' Kelvin went to the mask, picked it off the wall and turned it over. 'No, this is Giovanna. It says so right here.'

'Weird!' Helen sighed. 'Right, I need lunch, a pastry isn't going to cut it. I need a proper Italian. I'm fed up with Ealing High Street's version of authentic Italian cuisine, and anyway I can't think straight, I've clearly had too much sleep.'

*

For the next twenty minutes they meandered hand in hand along the winding paths that ran between the trullo houses. It was a scenic and well-kept town. Half of its citizens were clearly proud of their ancestry and the others, those that relied on the tourist industry, made sure that the streets were an Italian idyl.

Many of the restaurants were closed, being off-season, but they found a busy trattoria away from the tourist centre.

Kelvin was animated, chatting away with the waiters and fellow diners. The food was delicious, and Helen was made up, memorising the menu and the tastes so she could recount the experience to everyone at work.

The wine flowed, and being in holiday mode, they managed to polish off a bottle, in time to welcome and accept the complementary alcoholic digestive offered with the bill.

Their stroll back was impeded by a lack of focus, but

they were in no rush. They'd had a delicious lunch and had left the restaurant to find a majestic pink and purple sky, with the sun making its rapid descent. The new chill in the air sobered them slightly, enough to plan an attempt at getting the stove to work on their return.

As they drew near to Luigi's old home, they were surprised to find a group of five men and women in black, outside the trullo, dressed as if heading for a funeral. It was cold but not enough to explain their attire: low hats and high scarves. It was strange to see them just standing there, and although Kelvin tried to engage them in conversation, only one acknowledged them with a begrudging buonasera.

Kelvin and Helen quickly went inside.

'What is wrong with these people?' Helen said.

'Well, I'm getting used to it now. They were alright this morning and pretty friendly in the restaurant, so we can't complain. Tea?'

Kelvin was reaching for the saucepan to heat the water when they both heard it: a joyful giggling, which would have been delightful, but it seemed to come from somewhere in the house.

Kelvin turned off the tap to hear better. He looked at Helen and she raised an eyebrow. Kelvin resumed his tea making and then they heard it again, this time followed by the sound of talking.

'Buonasera, anyone there?' Kelvin called out, but they only heard the silence.

'This house gives me the creeps,' Helen said, picking up the order of service for the funeral, and for the first time noticing there was a picture of Luigi on the back. Was it a photograph of Luigi or a mask in his likeness?

'Right, I'll light the stove,' Kelvin said, and went

through to the living room, wondering if it was too early to start on the grappa, or whether he should have a little lie down first. He kneeled in front of the stove and the practicalities of lighting it came into focus. Where was the wood? Where were the matches? Probably in Luigi's studio. He got up and walked through to the guest bedroom. With a start, he saw that Helen had put the second skeleton together and dressed it, leaving it on the bed next to Luigi. 'Wow, you did that quickly,' he called out. 'Mine took at least twenty minutes.' He collected the mask from the living room and offered it up to the skeleton, where it snapped into place. 'Let's call this second one Giovanna,' Kelvin called out.

'Kelvin, come here.'

'God, not again.' Kelvin walked back to the kitchen.

Helen was holding her phone up, with the video of the funeral service to the newspaper cutting on the wall. 'It's Giovanna.'

'You mean it looks like Giovanna.' He poured himself a grappa. 'Anyway, well done for putting Giovanna together this morning, you should have said. I've put her mask on and I'm calling her Giovanna. Mine took ages; you did yours really quickly.'

Helen looked horrified, her mouth open, 'What are you talking about?'

'Putting the skeleton together, while I made breakfast, well, coffee.'

'I brushed my teeth,' Helen's voice had become shrill. 'I left the skeleton on the wall.'

'No, you're not getting me,' Kelvin said. 'Look, come through.'

Helen followed Kelvin to the guest bedroom and saw Luigi and Giovanna on the bed.

Helen didn't say anything. She didn't want to say it. Kelvin didn't want to say it.

'They're both dressed for a funeral,' Helen finally said. 'And they're both wearing their wedding rings. Where did you find those? Kelvin, is this a wind up?'

'Is what a wind up?'

'I left the pelvis on the bed, and I didn't find any wedding rings.'

'Helen! If you didn't put Giovanna together, who did?'

'I'm getting out of here.'

Kelvin followed Helen out to the kitchen. 'Hang on, there'll be an explanation.'

They heard the guest bedroom door softly close.

Helen looked at Kelvin and froze. Kelvin knocked back his grappa.

They heard it again, the giggling.

Helen walked slowly to the living room, stepping only just over the threshold.

She put her finger to her lips and pointed to the bedroom door. They could hear muffled voices, then the sound of passionate kissing and noises of satisfaction.

'That's not coming from another house,' Helen said.

Kelvin looked in horror. He didn't want to reply to Helen. 'Kelvin, it's coming from that bedroom,' Helen said loudly. Suddenly the noise stopped. They heard the bed squeak and footsteps walk to the door. The key turned in the lock.

'That's it!' Helen said. 'I'm out of here.'

'Helen, we can't just leave, what about our stuff?'

'Kelvin, there's someone or something in this house.'

Helen didn't stay to hear Kelvin's response; she grabbed her coat and handbag and was out the front door in seconds.

Kelvin stood and looked at the locked bedroom door. He was torn between following Helen or rescuing their possessions. He made a dash for their bedroom, fretfully calculating how much time he had.

Outside, Helen found the group of men and women had grown, there must have been thirty of them, all dressed in cloaks, and many wore Covid masks. She hadn't seen those in over a year. A priest in his vestments approached her and flicked a phial at her, droplets of water covered her face, which shocked her further. Many of the men and women were genuflecting.

The group quickly surrounded her and pushed her into their fold.

'Where is your husband?' the priest said.

'Inside.'

'Why did you come out?' the priest pressed.

Helen had to concentrate. Weird had just got weirder and she was struggling to understand. 'There's someone inside we didn't invite.'

The priest nodded and immediately, four men went into the house, one carrying a sledgehammer.

*

Kelvin had opened the two flight cases on the bed and was throwing their possessions in. He heard the front door open: was it Helen returning? He ramped up his speed.

But then two men came through into the bedroom door. The first one looked at him as if assessing whether he was a threat. 'We go,' he commanded Kelvin.

Kelvin didn't answer, but instead started zipping up the cases. The two men took over and lifted the cases off the bed. One walked out and the other stood behind Kelvin waiting for him to follow the other. In the living room Kelvin found the other two men.

'Who inside?' one of them said, pointing to the guest room door.

'I don't know.'

On hearing that, the man took his sledgehammer and smashed the door next to its handle. The wood splintered. He swung the hammer again and this time punched through. Another man put a hand through and twisted the key, then pushed open the door.

Everyone looked inside. Kelvin was peering over the four men's shoulders and saw the dressed and motionless wooden skeletons of Giovanna and Luigi embracing. He froze in disbelief, trying desperately to comprehend what was happening.

The first man nodded to the others and said to Kelvin, 'We go.'

Within seconds Kelvin was outside and shocked to find the silent mob. Their shuffling feet corralled him towards Helen and the priest. He smelled the chill of the air and the acrid scent of petrol. About fifteen of them carried wooden poles with petrol-soaked rags wrapped around the top.

The priest put his hand on Kelvin's shoulder. 'Is the house empty? Is there anyone inside?'

'Yeah, it's empty.'

The priest put both his arms in the air. 'In nome di Dio,' he shouted, and brought his arms down.

One man lit his torch from a lighter and the others offered their torches up to its flame. The man with the sledgehammer started to smash the windows of the trullo. One by one the torches, ablaze and belching black smoke, were hurled into the house through the broken windows. Smoke began to pour from the trullo, followed by sparks and finally a roaring fire.

The priest turned to Kelvin. 'They told me you were speaking in dialect this lunchtime. Where did you learn to speak our language with such a perfect accent?'

Kelvin looked terrified. 'I don't know, I don't speak Italian.'

The priest took out his phial of Holy water and sprinkled Kelvin. It was all too much for Kelvin, and he fainted into the arms of Helen.

*

Kelvin came around and found himself in bed in an unfamiliar room, with Helen next to him. 'Where are we?'

'They brought us to a hotel. We're not far from Luigi's home.

'Luigi's ex-home.'

'Hmm, yeah, not much of that left now,' Helen said quietly.

'Did I get all our stuff?'

'You did pretty well, just my heels and a dress missing. I think you left your phone charger though.'

'Not too bad then.'

'No.'

Kelvin stretched out. 'I'm thirsty.' Helen passed him a glass of water, which he gulped back.

'Yeah, but I think I could do with a real drink.' Groggily he sat up and picked up the receiver of the telephone on the bedside table. 'Hello, yes, do you have room service?' The receptionist spoke but Kelvin didn't understand. 'It's alright, I'll leave it.' He put the receiver down.

Helen was chuckling and smiling.

'What?'

'It's good to see you back to normal.'

Mary McKinnon: Launched into Eternity

Epigraph

Injustice anywhere is a threat to justice everywhere.

Martin Luther King, Jr.

Chapter One

I'm reading sociology at Bristol University. Apparently, that statement provokes an emotional response in most people. Being in my third term I'm still trying to fully appreciate that, but the more practical elements of life have been at the forefront of my focus. How to make an omelette that is more yellow than brown? How to make my loan last the term without the hungry bit at the end? How to tell if someone likes you or just wants an intimate knowledge of your underwear?

When I chose sociology, it was because my parents had. They'd met at uni all those decades ago, at a party with lots of drugs and people playing guitar, and making so much noise the Police were called. Then they'd gone back to Mum's room and had a lot of sex; this is the detail Dad emphasises. They'd stayed together from that point on without straying—the detail Mum emphasises. They'd watched their friends consume a succession of people. Meat, Dad calls them, possible suitors Mum says. "We got lucky and met early on", Dad says. "Don't settle down too quickly, you want to enjoy your mistakes", Mum says…usually after a few glasses of Pinot Grigio.

Now, when my parents' friends ask, sociology is the subject I was born to study. "I don't understand how you could get through life, or even want to, without studying people and why they behave the way they do." From my parents' male friends, I get encouraging smiles and enthusiastic conversation. "That's great Sophie, you've gotta love what you do". From their female friends I get silence and blank faces and then when I've finished ranting comes the quiet advice: "Get a good technical qualification love. People pay you for what you know and can make happen. When you're rich and independent then you can follow your interests." At uni I don't have these polite conversations. Sociology students are seen as slightly deviant and the subject area way too woolly to be truly academic.

It was only week six of the term and my bank balance was slipping into double digits. I work part-time, shelf-stacking, and am considering increasing my hours, but my current work commitment is already interfering with my studies.

This term I'd selected a module entitled 'A Socio-cultural Analysis of Prostitution for a Transformation in our Justice System'. The course was probably designed by one of our ancient dons who'd missed their political campaigning in the seventies and harnessed their defiant sense of humour and Machiavellian bent to create the greatest opportunity for heated debate, soul searching and existential crisis. Even the title was conflagratory for most of my fellow students. It should have been an analysis of sex working; the word prostitution was in the realm of the patriarchy.

It was an interfaculty, interdisciplinary module. Half of us were hard-core sociology students but the rest were studying law. It turns out we don't have much in common. Their sentiment is that we, that's me and my lefty-liberal friends, enjoy all shades of grey and prefer to share words and feelings rather than ever create solution-based policy and the sustainable development of our legal system, spending our term avoiding deadlines, study and the Establishment. Whereas they, the legal-eagle cohort, reside in a world of black and white, working ridiculously long hours, learning case law and legislation that's out of date and a mere framework to oppress anyone that doesn't earn the salary they're planning on having.

In week one of the term, we'd learnt that the "inter" part of the course would not include any mixing of "us" and "them", and in the lecture hall, the coffee bar and even the hallway there was a clear delineation. Fortunately, it was easy to steer this line, because there was a happy, coincidental difference in our dress code. I don't like to judge, but the general theme was we were more colourful, less branded, more vintage, less ironed, more floral, less groomed, definitely no ties, no brogues and no jackets. That's for the professors, right?

In week six, however, I made a transgression and fraternised with a boy studying law. I'd noticed that he'd make sure to ask the lecturer a question at the end of the lecture, but in such a way as to show off his knowledge. To be fair, he dressed somewhat ambiguously. He wore shoes that could be polished, but they were more red than brown. There was a jacket, but the collar was rakishly frayed. His hair had a parting but there were curly bits over his ears. I fancied him, I admit it, and I'd noticed him waiting outside the lecture hall since week one. I think it was his hubris and social energy that was the real turn on. He spoke with everyone, in complete violation of the known behavioural customs, refusing to be an "us" or "them". A social chameleon with an honest smile that needed no translation: I don't want to have to chase women, I'd like to dance a bit, before we fall into bed.

On the day of our first meeting, I'd worn my retro A-line mini with its massive rose print, put my hair up like Mum used to, and wore my purple danglies. Maybe I was overdressed for a lecture, but I was determined that he was going to notice me, and if he liked brunettes then how could he not talk to me? I stood in the spot where he always waited, and he was bang on time.

'Hey, nice dress.'

'Thanks, nice jacket.'

His eyes explored the rest of me.

'I've not seen you here before, are you new on the course?'

I crossed my arms and mocked annoyance. 'Shocking! It just goes to prove you have to dress up to be noticed.'

He chuckled, 'Wait, are you the girl-'

'Woman,' I corrected.

'Woman, that sometimes wears those cord dungarees and red woolly jumper?'

'Hmm, so you did notice.'

'You can't blame me for being discombobulated, it's quite a stylistic change.'

The door opened, and everyone started to wander into the lecture hall.

'I can blame you for identifying me with my dress sense and not simple facial recognition.'

'Well, where is a man supposed to look nowadays? Should he show an interest and give offense or ignore and give offense?'

'It's your responsibility to know when it's appropriate.'

He chuckled again. 'I agree. My father told me being appropriate is more important than being right…sometimes.'

He'd followed me down the stairs, and after I sat in my usual seat I looked around and he was right next to me.

'I'm Hugo, law, Badock Hall.'

'Nice to meet you Mr Law.'

'It's Crichton, Hugo Crichton.'

He looked worried. I laughed. 'I'm Sophie. Just Sophie

for now, and you don't need to know where I live… just yet.'

He gave me a forlorn smile, but I think he was impressed with my defiance. 'And sociology, yes?'

'Sociology major, English minor.'

'Nice combo.'

As we sat down, I saw Dr Rossi walk up the steps to the stage. She has a reputation for picking on people if they aren't concentrating and the auditorium hushed to hear her speak. I've read her book on digital sociology; she's a smart cookie and you don't want to get caught out. She barks with a strong Australian accent, so we call her Aussie Rossi.

Hugo and I gave each other a smile which said: talk later.

'Good afternoon, everyone. For those who've read ahead on your reading list you'll know today is the day we examine the case of Mary McKinnon.'

I looked around. There weren't many faces registering recognition and I couldn't remember where my reading list was.

'Oh! That is a shame.' She sighed loudly. 'Mary McKinnon should be thought of as your go-to example of rough justice, of patriarchal prejudice, a jury with obnoxious duplicity, victim blaming, slut shaming,' her voice grew louder, 'blatant male collusion, cultural intolerance to sex working, societal fear of female emancipation, and institutionalised sexism.' Arms crossed with dramatic pause. 'Let me tell you a story,' she chuckled, 'because that's what this is. The facts in this court room drama of murder do not meet the standards of a proper trial.'

At this point I was conscious of Hugo staring at me, or

my boobs anyway. But he looked up and caught my eye. He was unabashed, smiled and turned his eyes to Aussie Rossi.

Dr Rossi told us the story of Mary McKinnon, who was infamously hung for the murder of William Howat in 1823, when she was just 28. He was, reportedly, a client; a client of the intimate variety that is. But according to some witnesses he was not known to her at all. Dr Rossi began with the backstory, of how, after Mary's mother had died, her father had brought prostitutes back to the family home blatantly disregarding the presence of his then very young daughter. Of how Mary had then fled her abusive father and worked as a prostitute in order to survive.

Her fortune changed, arguably for the better, and she successfully opened a tavern and lodging house, under her own license. The tavern, however, was in the South Bridge district of Edinburgh, effectively an underground establishment. Not only because the sexual services offered in such establishments were a clandestine operation, but the premises themselves were physically in the dark, a mere vault in the bridge.

The rooms would have been damp, with little ventilation or natural light and Mary would have selected the accommodation because it had been abandoned or the rent negligible.

Despite being one of the oldest professions in the world, sex working had only really started in Edinburgh in the 1760s, but by the 1820s the South Bridge area was notorious for lodging houses providing extra services. Mary's business was thriving. Indeed, she was so successful that she could afford to have a night out with her friends on a Saturday, the busiest night of the week. Maybe it was this fact alone that led to her downfall.

William Howat had been drinking all day with his friends and had come to South Bridge to enjoy the comforts of Mary's tavern. His friends were shown into a room with a bed and a sofa and were being entertained by two of Mary's tenants/employees. When it came to payment, the mood turned violent.

Mary was called back to the tavern, and she attempted to resolve the fracas, but in vain. Within the hour William lay in hospital dying from a stab wound and Mary was in custody for attempted murder. William and his cohorts said it had been Mary who had held the knife. Mary and her lodgers did not have a coherent or consistent explanation.

At the end of the trial the judge directed the jury to give more weight to the testimony of the men over the women, as the women's trade and their obviously licentious disposition meant they lacked virtue, and consequently lacked credibility. Indeed, the judge told the jury to completely ignore one of the key witnesses in Mary's defence.

I caught Hugo's eye again and we both grimaced. I turned back again and saw that Dr Rossi was looking right at me.

'The jury reached a decision in only twenty minutes, finding Mary guilty of murder. What do we need to prove murder? Anyone?' Dr Rossi was waiting for an answer.

I had a shock when Hugo answered immediately. 'Actus reus and mens rea are essential for proving criminal responsibility,'

'Which are?'

Hugo didn't hesitate. 'A guilty act and a guilty mind,'

'And what is missing here?'

'She can't have intended to kill William Howat. She

didn't know him and the injury was inconsistent with attempted murder.'

'Very good, you'll go far.'

Hugo leaned back, pleased with himself. I tried to catch his eye, but he was focusing on Dr Rossi.

'How did a jury reach a conclusion so quickly?' She shook her head in disgust. 'They'd already made their mind up. We should be thankful, however, that they did recommend mercy.' She left another dramatic pause. 'Which is?'

Hugo hardly left a gap. 'They meant that Mary shouldn't be hanged.'

'Very good, or as they liked to say back then, "launched into eternity". What's your name?' she said, looking at Hugo.

'Hugo Crichton, Doctor Rossi.'

'You're very quick, but for the next question, let everyone else catch up and give them a chance.' She smiled.

Hugo nodded and grinned back.

'This call for mercy was based on the fact that Mary had no intention of killing, that the men who went to the tavern were violent, and because Captain James Brown, a superintendent who knew Mary and her family, said Mary was of a humane and pleasant disposition.'

I breathed a sigh of relief. I'd felt an impending sense of doom and was caught up in Mary's plight. Again, I looked at Hugo and he smiled back. A smile which seemed to say, poor Mary, how awful for her. He was going to be a lawyer, and justice was important to him.

'Within two months, Mary was hung, at a place they call the Lawn Market.' She took two steps to face the right side of the auditorium. 'You can go there today, there's a brass plaque.' She took two steps to the left. 'About twenty thousand people watched that day. It was 8.30 in the morning, but they weren't going to miss *a good hanging*.'

The auditorium was silenced. Aussie Rossi milked it, and I was angry with her for that. She'd led me up the proverbial garden path, thinking Mary would just serve a prison sentence, but then bashed me on the head with the garden spade. Mary was dead, at just twenty-eight.

I felt a bit tearful, pathetic I know, and Hugo saw and squeezed my hand, which kind of made me want to cry more. Pathetic, pathetic, pathetic. What a cruel world we live in.

Dr Rossi went on for another hour, and by the end I was emotionally shattered. She knew how to make us angry, sad and politically energised, bringing about change. I guess that's the point of the course. It's working.

I needed to go back to my halls and rest, shower and eat, put on my fave playlist, dance and open the Grey Goose. But Hugo suggested coffee and that was a more immediate reprieve, and maybe I just needed to talk it through. Plus, it was kind of exciting going to coffee with the star student—and a sexy one at that.

We went to the Source café; it's only a couple of hundred metres from the lecture hall. I made sure I bought my own coffee as I didn't want him thinking I was a freeloader. I pushed back into the plush purple cushions and tried to relax.

Hugo was on the edge of his chair. 'You were really shocked.'

'Weren't you? I mean, what a story.'

'Sophie, what you should know about me is that I always do my homework. I'd already read about Mary.'

I chuckled 'So that's why you had the answers.'

'You've got to do the reading anyway, no point in leaving it. The library's got some cool material. There's a pamphlet that was published for the day of the hanging. It includes a portrait that was painted of Mary while she was in gaol. Then there's a song that was made up about Mary's story, starting with her crap childhood and ending with the hanging. The crowd sang it on the day she was hung. Shockingly distasteful, so prurient, so vile.'

'She was impressed with you, Dr Rossi.'

'Exactly. I've made an impression. When she reads my essay, she's already formed an opinion of me. My career has already started. I'm on the treadmill. It's different for us.'

By that he meant my career as a sociologist, or whatever my career might be, was on the backburner.

Hugo pushed, 'You really felt for Mary?'

'Yeah, it's shocking. To be so young. All she was doing was defending her friends. It sounded awful, the loss of her mum, her abusive dad, the living conditions in the vaults.'

'Yeah, I read up about those. It was truly depraved, people living in conditions worse than stables. There was a problem with the construction of South Bridge. The horse and cattle manure that got dropped on the bridge as they passed, the human excrement too which was thrown into the street each night, it found its way from the road surface of the bridge and trickled down through the cheaply constructed, leaky masonry. The vaults underneath had stalactites of effluent. It was a living hell for them, that's the only reason Mary McKinnon could afford to have her own place. The vaults attracted the bootleggers and their illegal stills, and then there were the body snatchers, gangs of thieves raiding cemeteries for dead bodies to sell to medical students.'

'Why?'

'There was a shortage of bodies. Only the bodies of executed criminals could be used for dissection, and the price the body snatchers could get for one body was equivalent to a year's wages. But the cemeteries became too carefully guarded and so a new crime started: killing people just to sell their bodies. These were Mary's neighbours.'

'But do we have all the facts? It was a long time ago. Maybe she was in one of the tenement houses?'

'True, but either way you have to admit she took a great risk, working in that area.'

'You mean as a sex worker, or in that part of town?'

'Both.'

'Did she have a choice?'

Hugo grinned, 'Sophie, everyone always has a choice.'

Where was Hugo going with this?

'Sex workers today,' he continued, 'have a choice. For some the alternatives are dire, but they do exist.'

I considered Hugo afresh. The future of us might just have taken a different direction. I looked at him coldly. I needed to know if I should pick up my coffee and leave. 'Do you think the judge was wrong directing the jury as he did?' I managed to keep the heat out of my voice, but I think Hugo knew this was a test.

'No, he was clearly prejudiced. But here's the thing: was Mary or anyone else surprised about his prejudices? Wasn't that another risk she was taking?'

He was right if course, and I had to nod my agreement.

'It's not as though much has changed today,' Hugo continued, 'the Police routinely dismiss the testimony of sex workers. If they complain of assault or rape they're far from understanding.'

Just then I saw some of my friends collecting their coffees from the server. I have regular seminars with two of them. One of them I've known since the first day of uni. I waved instinctively; they waved back. Normally they would have come over and sat with me, but I could see they were heading towards the other side of the room. They'd clocked Hugo of course. I hoped they decided to sit somewhere else because they were giving us time to get to know each other, but maybe it was because Hugo wasn't our sort. I couldn't process it fast enough; Hugo was looking at me for an answer.

'They need to change the law and allow sex workers to work together.' I said. 'There's safety in numbers, and they can hire security. If it's above board it can be regulated, and they can be protected. The law drives them underground and that attracts criminal behaviour.' I'd gushed that out, it was well rehearsed.

'And are those your views or are they your fellow...'

God, what was he going to say? I put my hand on my coffee, ready to walk.

'Your fellow sociologists'? I mean, how far do you want to go with liberalisation? A knocking shop on every high street corner?'

'I want sex workers to be respected for the choices they make and not be demonised or dehumanised.'

Hugo was mulling it over and swigging his coffee. Perhaps he was he giving me time to calm down.

'I guess what strikes me about Mary's case,' he continued, 'is that it was a male, female thing, wasn't it? About whether a woman has the right to use her body as she pleases. That judge wanted women in the home looking after babies, making meals for their husbands, not profiteering from and exploiting men's weaknesses. He wanted to punish Mary for her afront to the male order.'

I was pleasantly shocked. 'Yeah, absolutely.' I said, warmly, 'Hmm, you are a thinker, and not just a pretty face.' I chuckled.

He was looking at my boobs again, and I quite liked where this could be heading. He'd pushed the sleeves of his jumper up, exposing his muscular forearms. Then I noticed his lips were full and a little more red than usual. I imagined him kissing me, using his tongue on our first kiss.

'So, there's just one problem,' Hugo said. 'You know, about the moral territory of this. As a lawyer—future lawyer, in the criminal courts anyway, I'll be looking to influence the opinion of the jury, and I just want to dig down into the point about cultural intolerance.'

Huh, now he was sounding all pompous. I wished he was a little more consistent.

If someone,' Hugo continued, 'does something which others think is wrong, are those others right to assume that the perpetrator's integrity is questionable? That from one misdeed, the others can infer a host of other actions they might have performed, particularly if there is little evidence?'

I looked at my friends drinking coffee, hoping they couldn't hear our conversation. Part of me wanted to agree with Hugo, part of me thought I should be calling him a dick and leaving. I was genuinely conflicted. Did he have a point?

'Mary sold beer,' Hugo continued, 'hired rooms to women that she knew would exchange intimate physical services for cash. Maybe they gave hand jobs, maybe it was full intercourse, we don't know.'

God! Why did he have to detail it?

'But Mary's income,' Hugh continued, 'came indirectly

82

from that activity. And maybe Mary too made a quick buck on the side with the punters she liked, or the one's that she couldn't palm off on her lodgers.' Hugo frowned and looked at me. 'I guess if that was you, I'd be running a mile, but I don't think you're like that at all, which is why I'm here. I think you're the kind of girl who has what you'd call integrity.'

Ugh! Why did he have to go and spoil it? Wow, but wasn't he good? I wanted to agree with him, to be the girl that he would think well of, but I didn't want to agree with him for the fear of abandoning Mary and what she stood for: the right to use her body as it suited her and not be enslaved to Victorian misogynistic values.

'You've made your point articulately, that's your job, isn't it? Or will be.'

I looked at Hugo's hands. They looked muscular, dexterous and for some bizarre reason, imagined them on my breasts. Concentrate, Sophie! 'Isn't it more complicated than that? We certainly don't want jurors who think only in black and white. We need them to be able to cope with conflicting truths and not have a knee jerk reaction based on some borderline cultural bias.'

Hugo was smiling at me, but it didn't seem sarcastic.

'What!' I said.

'No, I like it: beauty and brains. Go on, please.'

'Okay, well what about your integrity as a lawyer? If you have a hunch a defendant is guilty, or in fact you know they're guilty, do you still defend them? How many lawyers turn down a case because they're worried about the effect on their integrity?

Hugo was nodding his head, smiling and chuckling. He reached out his hand and slowly brought it down behind me and rubbed my shoulder, in a kind of, 'I like you' type way. I could have shrugged it off, but I liked it.

Then I got a shock.

'Sophie, you may think this an outrageous suggestion, but what do you think about you and I going up to Edinburgh this weekend and checking it out? It would look like proper field research for our essays. We could go in my Dad's Lotus and stay at an Airbnb. I've read so much about the case, and I'd love to experience it in the flesh.'

Hugo was looking at his coffee as he was speaking, which was just as well, as I don't think I could have hidden my expression. But then he turned directly to me, and I had to wear my best poker face.

'Listen,' he continued, 'you're probably thinking I'm a little forward, but truth is, I've been watching you for a few weeks. No, sorry, that does sound a little creepy. But hey, I'm attracted to you, and maybe this is the most honest way of showing you that-'

'Yes,' I said.

'Yes?' Hugo repeated.

'Yes, I'd like to go up to Edinburgh with you.

Hugo raised his coffee cup, and I chinked it with mine.

Chapter Two

Hugo picked me up from my halls of residence at silly o'clock, way before breakfast time. He said he's a morning bird and naturally wakes at this time to begin his studies.

His dad's Lotus was an Emira v6. I'm not really passionate about cars, but I knew this was special and Hugo was clearly well practised in driving it. Right from the start he showed off with an acceleration that made my back press into the bucket seat. After half an hour he relaxed, explaining that a speeding ticket could affect his chances of being a judge one day.

His Max Verstappen act was then replaced with an embodiment of Scott Mills as we listened to his road trip playlist through the Emira's immersive sound system.

For the first time that morning I began to relax. We couldn't have a conversation over the volume Hugo had set, and I got the impression he just wanted to concentrate on his driving and enjoy the ride.

Where was he in his head? It must be quite a thrill taking a woman away on a weekend in a sports car. Did that make me a commodity, his arm candy? It was a good feeling to be the one chosen to sit in the passenger seat of a sleek, glossy symbol of excess and all things luxurious. It didn't matter whether I did or didn't fit the lifestyle. I was here, I was the chosen one. Where would Hugo like me next? Draped over the bonnet in my underwear? I imagined him giving me some haute couture Parisian lingerie, wrapped in a subtle black box tied with a lace ribbon, with just a wink and a nod that meant 'wear it tonight, so I can take it off later'.

Actually, this was quite surreal. I'd only told one of my

friends, Poppy, that I was going to skip town on a field trip. She'd seen me in the coffee bar and didn't vocalise her judgement, she just didn't look me in the eye. That told me she was a) worried and b) doubtful of my choice. After all, hadn't we spent the term making disparaging comments about the shallowness of law students, pigeonholing them as culturally skewed. At our most mean, we compared them to a Frankenstein marriage of David Cameron suture-stapled to Donald Trump, "without anaesthetic please".

Having said that, Hugo was what my mother called marriage material: confident, articulate and monied. Not that they were ever likely to meet. I hadn't brought home any of my boyfriends from uni and I was well into the first year. But I can hear Mum saying, 'Sophie, you've got a keeper there. He's committed to his studies, and a career at the Bar.' She'd mean of course in the courts, not the pub, and Dad would crack the joke and Hugo would look at his feet, appalled. No, I couldn't imagine taking Hugo home anytime soon. Wasn't he out of my league anyway? I've been choosing between eating or a night out drinking; selecting a new pair of shoes, not because I want a change of colour, but because I'm fed up with a soggy foot every time it rains.

Wouldn't socialising with Hugo be a constant embarrassment? What would his parents make of me in my upcycled, charity shop fashion? His dad might give him some extra allowance to buy me something more 'presentable'. Cringe! Hugo's father was a judge, after all. Hugo's clear ambition.

I contemplated trying to make conversation around the dining room table and being lost in the spurious dropped names of celebrities and esoteric courtroom gossip.

Hugo turned the music down. 'So where shall we start

our research?' He turned and winked.

Was that a wink or a wink and a nudge, a euphemism? 'There's so much to see,' I said, 'Mary McKinnon related or otherwise. We could go and find her grave?'

Hugo chuckled. 'You didn't hear about her dissection then.'

I didn't reply but imagined Mary in her cell contemplating her fate. To be sliced and carved up by a group of men, no doubt playing with her body and if not mocking it, then treating it with utter contempt.

'They say her friends tried to keep it from her,' Hugo continued, 'you know, when they visited her in gaol, but she must have known.'

I needed to change the subject.

'Sorry,' Hugo said. 'Not very romantic of me.' He turned the music back up.

That made it awkward. I didn't like to be silenced with that thought. I turned the music down. 'Let's start by walking up the Royal Mile, that's the must-see tourist destination.'

Hugo nodded and I turned up the music.

"Romantic", Hugo had said. Another surreal moment. I'd never done this before, a weekend away with sex as part of the itinerary. Hugo was hot, and that was what university was all about, wasn't it? Sexual experimentation. But until Hugo had said the word romantic, I guess I was uncertain about what was on the schedule.

After his suggestion in the coffee bar, we'd only had a brief phone call about where we'd stay. "What kind of place do you want to stay in?" he'd asked. It was open ended and I stumbled with ers and ums. Thoughts had raced through my head: was he asking whether we should share a room, a bed? Was he talking about whether I wanted a spa complex or inhouse dining? In the end I blurted out, "I'll check if there's a Youth Hostel up there."

His reply was immediate. "No, I'll book an Airbnb. You put in what you'd pay for a hostel, and I'll find the rest."

So, Hugo using the word romantic was a relief. I knew what we would be doing, what might be on the agenda. But there weren't many other clues. There was little flirtation, no kiss when he greeted me and put my weekend bag in the ridiculously tiny boot. No wandering hand between changing gears. No inuendo. I mean, I'd freak out if he'd turned up with chocolates and flowers and opened the door for me, but this was lacklustre.

Maybe this was just how his lot did this kind of thing. My previous uni boyfriends had not set the bar particularly high. From my first I learned that the hygiene standards I held universal were for some too high and difficult to achieve. The second had an annoying habit of assuming that my calendar and unscheduled time was for him to populate. Hugo, it seemed, was a completely different kind of animal. Maybe we'd just meet up on skiing holidays, and official dates while he immersed himself in his studies. That was one thing he'd made clear last night: he wouldn't be studying this weekend, he'd leave the books behind and have a proper holiday.

'Good, let's leave our books behind,' I'd said.

'Well, maybe I'll take one small volume, that and some aftershave, my briefest briefs and a sense of adventure.'

That was the last I'd heard from him before he collected me seven hours later.

Norwich to Edinburgh was supposed to be six hours, but after a traffic jam, coffee and wee stops, mitigated by Hugo's heavy foot in the Lotus, it was more like seven.

It gave us time for some conversations between Hugo's playlists. We learned that neither of us had ever been to Edinburgh, indeed Scotland. But I was excited as I'd taken the module 'Social Issues in a Scottish Context' and Hugo explained how he was intrigued about visiting Edinburgh for his law degree, because they have a different legal system to England.

He gave me a short summary that covered their taxation system, conveyancing, devolvement, probate and divorce. He knew his stuff.

But maybe these motives were disingenuous, particularly the intention of finding out more about Mary. Maybe I was only looking to be wined and dined on a romantic weekend away, and Hugo was looking for the same with the added thrill of driving his dad's Lotus for an eight-hundred-mile round trip.

And where were the conversations we should be having, anyway? The recounting of anecdotes that displayed our values, a willingness to divulge personal histories, stories that led to laughter? Maybe I'd been reading too many sociology books, they're not a life manual after all.

Just after I pointed out the "Welcome to Scotland" sign, everything Hugo said was uttered with a thick Scottish accent.

'Ee lassie, it's cold now we're over the border. Maybe we'll get a little haggis to keep us warm.'

It was good, but I'm glad we weren't in public; it wasn't exactly p.c. Hugo impersonated every Scottish cliche you could think of. Out came all his petty hates and irritation with the Scottish people. It was funny, and that is the nature of comedy, it's not polite. But I'd have to make sure his impersonations stopped when we got out of the car.

The closer we got, the wetter and darker it became, and

as we reached the outskirts of Edinburgh black clouds threatened lightning, laying a drab curtain over the city centre's grandiose neo-Georgian buildings. Not the best start. To be fair, it was only mid-April. The buildings stood tall and statesmen like, as they should be for Scotland's capital. I Googled it; they're Craigleith sandstone. Sounds nice, but they're basically grey in the rain. The roads were molten silver, with the sky a moody veil of gloom - or was it doom? I knew it was only weather, but a shadow had been cast over our weekend.

I'd not asked Hugo directly where our hotel was. I suspected he wanted to surprise me with a dramatic gesture that matched his ego. I imagined a 5-star spa, something with room service. Wasn't that his style?

It was time to programme in the last part of the journey.

'What's the address? I'll put it into Maps,' I offered.

'Oh, don't worry, I know the way. I committed it to memory.'

'Come on Hugo, it's time for the big reveal.'

'It's just off South Bridge. We're nearly there.'

I remembered the name from somewhere. I didn't know why as I'd never been there, but it was an address I'd heard before. I looked out for the palatial front of a hotel, the columns of a royal edifice, something swanky, with a portico to drive under and drop off our baggage. Better still, a porter waiting for Hugo to hand over the keys and park the car for him. If you're going to dream, dream big.

Hugo began to slow down.

It didn't look right. 'Why are you stopping?'

'We're here.' Hugo had a big grin. 'You're going to love it, this is true oldy-worldy Edinburgh.'

We'd stopped in a cobbled side street behind a skip. Five-storey buildings hemmed us in. There might as well have been a sign saying, "Seedy Rooms Here".

'You're leaving the car here?' I couldn't take the hint of incredulity out of my voice.

'No chance, Dad would freak. We'll just drop the bags and I'll park up later. I've got an address for secure parking.'

I didn't really want to get out. The street had the feel of an ideal place for a nefarious transaction, swapping illegal substances for cash, waiting to be laundered. But Hugo was already out and had gone straight to a key safe next to a door with a rusty grid over its window. Great, the owner wasn't even here to let us in. Soon Hugo was holding the door open for me, looking at me with his cheeky grin. I opened the car door, not wanting to leave the comfort of its leather seats.

'Sophie, you're going to love it, its authentic. I'd say Dickensian, but I'm not sure Charles set a novel here.'

I was trying to evaluate whether loving an authentic Dickensian building was an oxymoron. 'We're not doing a hotel then?' I said, clutching at straws.

'It's an Airbnb experience, boutique, if you like. When I got back from the coffee bar, I Googled and found this straight away. Our room is called 'William Burke'.'

The Airbnb was a dive, with peeling paint and rusting door hinges. We climbed a staircase whose squeaks sounded like 'go home' and which was covered in a carpet with sticky bits. White walls a decade or so past needing a refresh. Hugo, though, seemed to think it funny. Why did he choose this dump? I would have put in a lot more if I'd known he'd decided to scrimp.

'This is just what I thought it'd be like,' Hugo chuckled. 'Proper ancient Edinburgh, sullied and characterful.'

At the top of the landing Hugo stopped. 'Here you go,

William Burke.' He opened the door, which had an even longer creak, long enough to sound like, 'You really do want to go home'. To be fair we were hit with the whiff of sandalwood and patchouli, when my expectations had been damp and rot.

Maybe he was right. I appraised the building again and took in the oak beams, the Arts and Crafts doorknobs and window handles, the stained glass above the room door. Who knows? Maybe they were genuine Mackintosh. And the bed was a fourposter. Is that why Hugo chose it? No drapery, but four solid posts and a foot and headboard that said, 'Finest Scottish oak'. It was carved with a mixture of Celtic rope patterns and unusual beasts. Demons and angels? Don't know, but Hugo was right: we'd booked character by the square foot.

The double bed began to consume my thoughts. This was now very surreal. When he'd promised to replace a youth hostel with something better, I wasn't sure exactly what he meant; and although this was definitely better, his assumption that we'd share a bed, was a thought that began to occupy more and more headspace.

I'd already transferred my share of the cost to Hugo, so I didn't want to splash out again and reserve my own bedroom. Do I raise it as a point of contention, I wondered? At least there was a sofa for him to offer to use. I guess if Hugo didn't become more romantic soon, I'd have to say something. I mean, what did he think was going to happen, that we'd just get into bed and make love? As Mum would say, I'd got myself into a pickle.

The fourposter bed did have a powerful alure. What is it about them that seems so safe and snug and sexy all at the same time? What fairytale had been told that I'd absorbed that connection? The bed clothes were amazing, this was surely where the budget had gone. The mattress was waist high, with a deep purple eiderdown. A heraldic shield of lions and roses was embroidered in the centre, bordered by a medieval shaped dragon, castellations, and knights and ladies with Arthurian coned hats. The pillows were stacked and numerous, yet in keeping with the theme. I drew a finger over the bedcover.

'Later,' Hugo said, walking to the window. Then he chuckled and pointed. 'That's a knocking shop if ever I saw one.'

I stepped over to stand next to him. 'How many have you seen?'

He didn't reply. Our Georgian property overlooked a main street.

'That's South Bridge,' Hugo said enthusiastically.

'South Bridge?'

'Oh Sophie!' He raised an eyebrow. 'The place where Mary McKinnon stabbed her client.'

Hugo had done his homework and then some.

I giggled. It was either that or cry. 'You chose this place because of the lecture?'

'Yeah, that's why we came isn't it? You wanted the real historical Edinburgh experience. You won't get that at the Hilton.'

I was finding it difficult to share Hugo's passion.

Look there goes another punter,' Hugo said, nodding towards the building opposite.

'You think it's a brothel?'

'Yeah, well it's in the right area of town. There are guys going in ones or twos. No girls going in.'

'It could just be a pub,' I said.

'Okay, it's just a hunch. We'll go and see later. Check out the quality of the merchandise.'

'Oh God you're awful, merchandise!'

Hugo chuckled. 'What else are you going to call them, lost souls?'

'Urgh, I can't believe you said that.' Was he joking?

Hugo walked to a kettle perched on a fridge outside the ensuite. 'Do you mind if I just chill for a bit. That journey was longer than I thought it would be.'

'Of course, you sit and relax. I'll make us a cuppa.'

Hugo sat on a sofa by the window, stretched out and looked at his watch. 'Actually, you know what would be good?' He picked up his rucksack, reached inside and pulled out one of his legal tomes. 'Just a quick read—honest.'

'All this way and you're going to read?'

'Just one chapter. I've got to a good bit.'

I frowned.

He put his glasses on and read out loud. 'A Comparison of Scottish and English Law since the Act of Union 1707.'

'I'll unpack, you enjoy. Tea or coffee?'

I put Hugo's coffee next to him and unpacked my little case into the chest of drawers.

'Don't worry, I'll unpack mine.' Hugo said, without looking up.

It must have been only twenty minutes that went by, but I was aching to actually see something of Edinburgh. We'd be heading back home in forty-eight hours.

'Come on Hugo, it's only two o'clock, let's get out and tick off something on the must be done sights of Edinburgh.'

Hugo stood up and dropped his book on the sofa. 'I'd rather take you to bed,' he said, putting his hands around my waist.

My heart raced, and the anxiety must have shown on my

face. 'I'm not going anywhere; I'll still be here after our little adventure.'

'Aye well if it's buildin's of Edinburgh you'd prefer,' Hugo said in a strong Scottish accent.

He walked to the window and pulled back the curtains, no doubt observing the brothel, if it was one. Then my words twirled around. I hadn't said 'no you can't take me to bed', or any other form of no. I'd said, "I'll still be here after our little adventure." Did I just negotiate my way into sleeping with him? I heard Mum saying, "Sophie, you're over-thinking again."

There was nothing for it, if I was going to get Hugo out of the room, I'd have to give an ultimatum. I put on my shoes. 'I'm taking my coat, just in case.'

Hugo just stood looking out of the window. What over-thinking was he doing?

'Oh, and I'll take the umbrella too, in case there's a big downpour.'

Finally, he spoke, 'I thought we'd get a bit of lunch. I've been given a couple of recommendations.'

'Sure, that would be nice, my budget runs to a sandwich.'

'Urgh, no, it's a weekend away. I'll get you lunch.'

Now I felt bad, forcing him to walk after his mega driving sprint and then forcing him to stroll around the damp, grey streets of Edinburgh. 'That would be lovely. I'm sorry if you're tired, after all that driving.'

'I'll think of a way you can make it up to me.'

I smiled as enthusiastically as I could. The truth was I'd have loved to be wined and dined but I didn't fancy being bribed into it. 'Shoes then?'

'Shoes?'

'Are you going to wear shoes?'

95

Chapter Three

Finally, we were out. The atmosphere in the dingy room was oppressive and made even the grey skies welcome. The room was at least central, so we were soon strolling along the Royal Mile. It was busy—lots of tourists no doubt; and the road was actually quite long, as its name promised.

I heard Hugo's phone ping with a notification and he checked it, not telling me what it was, and I didn't feel I could ask. But we were no longer strolling, and rather than Hugo languishing behind me, it was now me struggling to keep up with the stride of a man who was six feet two.

'Let's go and find the brass plaque,' Hugo said.

Good, at least he was enthusiastic. 'What brass plaque?'

'The place where all the executions took place.'

We came to the corner of George IV Bridge and the High Street, and Hugo was soon pointing. 'Look, here it is.'

The brass plaque was set into one of the magnificent state buildings that line the famous street, with its huge mullion stones, looking like a giant's stacked pillows. It read "Site of the last execution in Edinburgh. The site of the gallows is marked by three brass plates. George Bryce the Ratho murderer was executed here on 21st June 1864."

'Who's George Bryce?' Hugo asked.

'I don't know, but I guess we're in the right territory for Mary McKinnon.'

Hugo ran a finger over the plaque as I had done with the bed. Moments later, I nearly jumped out of my skin when I heard a shout behind me. I turned to find a young woman, our age, in a red dress, looking straight at Hugo and me.

'Aye, you've come for Mary McKinnon, have you? Prurient revellers in the fallen woman's demise.'

Her accent was strong and her skin very pale. Long black locks cascaded around her shoulders; it must have been a wig.

'We have, we have! Tell us more,' Hugo said.

Hugo was animated; it was as though someone had switched him on. The woman's red dress looked like a Victorian showgirl's costume, with a raised front permanently showing her legs, stockings and suspenders. She was beautiful, but her dress was shockingly inappropriate for the middle of the High Street. I didn't know where to look. Hugo did.

The woman put her hands on her hips and kicked out a foot. 'All you need to say is "Mary McKinnon" three times, and then, "get you to eternity, vile woman". And you will suffer the possession of Mary.' She let out a hideous cackle, too comedic to be frightening, or at least I thought so, but Hugo didn't laugh, he looked on, open mouthed.

By now, we were not alone. A crowd of people stood around us as if she were some kind of busker. I suspected Hugo would have had a comeback for such occasions, but he remained in a trance.

Then she put her hand up as if calling to the crowd. 'Mary McKinnon, Mary McKinnon, say it once more and that's three times to bring the curse. Put the rope round her throat, launch her to eternity, no mercy for Mary McKinnon.'

Maybe she was a stooge paid for by Edinburgh's Tourist Board. She was certainly captivating in her long, red, tartan dress with a black lace garter. Her hair was tied up in lace too.

'Mary, Mary, she's paid for the stabbin', now she'll get a hangin'.'

How long was this going to go on for? I pulled on Hugo's hand. I wanted to get away from her. Hugo squeezed my hand, and we headed off.

'Scary, huh?' Hugo said, smiling. 'Come on, let's find that restaurant, it's just up here: The Fat Angus.'

When we went through the restaurant door, I realised I was still holding Hugo's hand. I let go as inconspicuously as I could.

Hugo was masterful with the waitress, commanding that we had a table by the window. He quizzed her on the wine list and ordered a bottle of red straight away. It's not my favourite drink but I wasn't paying, and actually, I thought a glass might steady my nerves.

Hugo was in his element, reading the menu studiously, directing me to what would be good, and a better match with the wine, then suggesting I have a starter.

It was a delicious meal. His recommendation was well placed. The conversation, though, was firmly in the territory of stilted and unlike that of a date. I'm not an expert, but I've seen enough rom-coms and read enough trashy novels to know that Hugo either didn't fancy me or thought engaging with or entertaining me was unnecessary.

He drank heavily. I had more than a glass, but soon he was finishing the bottle. Out of the blue, his mood and honour depleted.

'You know Sophie, I have been to a brothel before,' he said, watching my reaction.

His eyes felt invasive, as if he wanted to see how upset he could make me.

'It was a stag thing.'

'I don't really need to know.'

'Well, I think you do, after all, isn't that why we're here?'

What is it with alcohol that makes people turn so quickly? His face was brutal, his eyes dark.

'All the guys had her, there and then, in the room. I mean, it was supposed to be just a lap dance, but you know how these things go. It was very obliging of her to take all of us.'

'I hope you gave her a good tip.'

'Oh yes, I did: Get a job.' Hugo snorted. He'd amused himself. 'Get a real job.' He chuckled, still reminiscing.

I was silent, but he was going to talk at me anyway, and I didn't fancy wrestling him for the door key to the Airbnb.

'She was well spoken, alert, well dressed, well at the beginning,' he chuckled again. 'She didn't need to take that job, Sophie, that's the point I'm making.'

'You defiled her with your words; before that, it was a business transaction.'

'She humiliated herself before we even started.' Hugo's voice was raised. His lips tight. 'She'd turned up to get broken.'

'She turned up to pay her bills.'

The waitress came. Maybe she thought Hugo had called her over when he'd raised his voice.

Hugo ordered another glass of dessert wine, in a broad Scots accent; she must have known he was putting it on as she'd taken our original order.

She confirmed the order in her very strong accent and Hugo had to ask her three times to restate what she'd said.

Finally, he repeated what she'd said, but sounding like King Charles. He was being a pig. I mouthed 'sorry' to her, and she nodded and walked off.

Hugo swigged back his wine. 'I fail to see how choosing to be a sex worker is an empowering choice. And for the feminist movement to champion that choice is a hopeless, if not curious, monstrous self-sabotage.'

Hugo was drunk, losing the plot.

I'd been caught off-guard, and Hugo was showing me the man he really was. Showing me his potential as a man at the Bar, manipulating the jury to feel moral outrage. I made up my mind: when I got back, I'd dump him, or finish whatever this was. There was no point in falling out now, it would be a long way back in the car with a bad vibe. I'd just try to enjoy the weekend as much as I could.

I must have zoned out.

'Sophie, any comeback?' Hugo was grinning. 'I'm playing devil's advocate.'

Or are you just being the devil? I thought.

'Oh, come on Sophie, you're not going to give up there are you?'

'I assume you are referring to Dolores French's book, but not all feminists agree with her. Many see prostitution as pure male exploitation.'

'There you go,' Hugo said, 'beauty and brains,' he left a dramatic pause, 'but still no integrity.'

'What do you mean, no integrity?'

'Because you're here, Sophie. You came away with a guy you'd only known for two hours to share a bed with him.'

'You booked a room with one bed, not me, and anyway, why does that mean, *I* have no integrity?'

'Well, it's a bit slutty, isn't it?'

'And you're not slutty?'

'Sophie, I'm a guy, I can't be slutty. You don't get it. You live in a society where you're getting judged, not me.

I get to sleep around; you have to be the virgin. Deal with it.'

'God, do you know, you're right. I really have let myself down, being here with you. But do you know what, I get to change. I can tell you where to get off. I have a choice.'

'Hallelujah, thank you!'

Hugo leaned back in his chair, arms behind his head in smug satisfaction.

'Oh God! What now?'

'Yes, Sophie, you have a choice. Just like Mary had. That's what I've been trying to show you. However bad it gets, you don't have to sell your body.'

I stood up, making it clear I'd had enough. Hugo grinned to himself and then staggered off to pay. I stood by the front door and watched as he used his phone. It looked as though he was answering a text.

Glancing outside, I saw a flash of lightening and shortly after came the rumble of thunder.

When we turned to leave, I was shocked to find the woman in the red tartan dress standing in the doorway, as if she'd been waiting for us.

'Hello you,' Hugo said.

'Hello, you. I must say you are looking very dapper tonight.'

Her wig had slipped a bit, and I could tell she was struggling in her high heels.

'And you're looking pretty lovely yourself.' Hugo's words were quite slurred. 'I really love your dress; I think they should make those mandatory.'

'Why, thank you, I'm glad you like it.'

'I'm Hugo, what's your name?'

'You can call me Mary,' she giggled, 'for tonight.'

It started to rain, which I took as a signal to go, and walked quickly in the direction of the Airbnb. It was actually a simple route and I didn't need Hugo to lead the way. I thought I'd leave them to it, but Hugo soon caught up with me. We walked in silence. I kept him slightly behind. But when we got to the plaque Hugo stopped, and shouted as loudly as he could, 'Mary McKinnon, Mary McKinnon, Mary McKinnon, get you to eternity, vile woman.'

I was several places ahead of him by the time he'd finished shouting, and then heard him struggling to catch up. He made a couple of attempts at conversation, but I ignored him. I didn't feel compelled to share my umbrella. After fifteen minutes, for some reason, I began to feel sorry for him, and waited for him.

'When do you think my possession kicks in?' Hugo chuckled.

'She said the curse is that you'll suffer the possession of Mary McKinnon, she didn't say you'll be possessed by her.'

Fortunately, that silenced him, as he tried to work it out. He looked quite forlorn with the rain slowly drenching him. The lightning lit up the pavement.

'Hang on, I like your distinction,' Hugo slurred, 'but what was Mary possessed by?'

'I don't know, it wasn't my bogus myth, but how about the possession of a feminist rage battling Georgian male misogyny? You'll suffer Mary's rage.'

'That was quick. Quick for you Soph.'

'It's Sophie to you.'

Before we turned the corner into Cowgate, I looked behind and saw the woman in red again. She briefly caught my eye, then turned away. Minutes later, when fumbling with the key to get in, I saw her at the end of the alleyway. It was as if she were checking up on us. Had she followed us? Or was she after Hugo? She could have him.

Once through the black wooden door I flicked the light switch. Nothing. 'Really!'

I pulled out my phone and wiggled it to operate the torch. We walked up the staircase in silence. There was a definite chill in the air that I hadn't felt outside. My torch seemed unable to light up much of our way and finding our door wasn't quick. Hugo struggled to turn the key. I just wanted to get inside and feel cosseted. But when the door opened, I didn't get that feeling. It was, if anything, colder. The streetlights outside our window barely lit the room. I tried the light switch; still nothing. Then I noticed a smell. Not musty or damp, but something else, like a dead rat.

'I'm going to have a shower,' Hugo said.

'In the dark?'

'Yeah, I know where everything is. I'll get my willy clean for you.'

Hugo was still drunk then.

'Don't bother on my account, you're not going anywhere near me.'

I hunted for a fuse box, holding my phone torch up against the wall. That's when I found the weirdest picture. I don't know how I missed it before. It was of a public hanging. Thousands of people gathered around a stage. The gallows prominent and a woman standing underneath the rope. I read the description, "Mary McKinnon Executed 16th April 1823". I looked at the picture again, there was a vicar or priest sitting and watching. I remembered the part from the lecture where she'd tried to talk to the crowd and explain who had stabbed William Howat, but no one had listened, and she'd given up.

I continued around the room, tripping over Hugo's case. Picking myself up I noticed a light fitting above the bed, but something about it was wrong. I stepped closer and held my torch up. The cord holding the light was tied in a hangman's noose. 'God, what is this place!'

Just then, I felt something touch my hand and yelped, surprised by both the cold and the thought that Hugo had crept in behind me. 'Your hands are like ice!' But Hugo didn't answer.

I looked around and realised Hugo was still in the shower. It must have been the door handle or something.

The room was just too creepy, too many shadows and too quiet, the ceiling too low, the curtains too thick. I heard the door slam at the bottom of the stairs and went to the window. A group of men were outside the supposed brothel laughing with the woman in red, who was pointing at our apartment window. I took a step back, not wanting to be seen. The room felt like a castle under attack. No, more like a prison cell. Quickly, I jumped up onto the bed and tucked my feet up.

Hugo came out of the shower, quietly, with just a towel around him. He stood a moment and then sat up on the bed, reaching out for me.

I backed away to the far edge.

'Oh, come on Soph, let's not waste the weekend.'

'Hugo, you've blown it.'

He reached out for me, and I had to push his hand away, putting a pillow between us. 'Keep to your side of the bed or else.'

'Woah!' Hugo did an impression of a mad Scottish ghost. 'I'll be damned to eternity.'

'No, you'll just get my knee between your legs.'

He barely gave a grunt before walking over to the

window.

'Hmm, there's that lovely woman, the one in the slutty dress.'

'I'm having a shower,' I said, and grabbed a towel.

'Yes, get good and clean for me.'

'In your dreams.'

The shower room was pitch dark, there wasn't even a window for a glimmer of light. I washed myself as best I could, fumbling for the shower gel, disorientated by the lack of shadow. But the water was hot and after ten minutes I felt warm again and refreshed.

When I came out of the shower enclosure, I called out for Hugo. I just needed to know where he was so I could avoid him. All I heard was the silence. I dried myself and dressed. Back in the bedroom, I called out again. He wasn't there.

'Hugo? Hugo?' No answer.

I got into bed, sitting up against the headboard. Why was the room so creepy? And why was the room called William Burke? I Googled it. "William Burke and William Hare were a pair of infamous murderers for profit, who killed their victims and sold the corpses to an anatomist for purposes of scientific dissection."

This place was someone's weird idea of a joke.

Then my screen went black; it was the battery. It felt like a tipping point, my prison cell becoming an open cage. I had no means of calling for help.

The rain was falling harder now and that meant I wouldn't be able to hear any footsteps on the stairs. Hugo might come back at any moment, so I couldn't take my clothes off to sleep. But I was tired from the wine and the early dawn departure, and the awful negative atmosphere with Hugo. It had been exhausting.

I reviewed the day: what a disaster. Hugo is, in fact, no better than William Howat. What breeds monsters like these men who think they can behave so badly?

I thought about going out to get my phone charged. Maybe just get a taxi to a better side of town. Then I realised I didn't know who had the key. I felt on top of the bedside table, the last place I'd seen it. Nothing. Hugo had the key. I couldn't go out and be sure of getting back in. Was there a deadlock? At least I'd know when Hugo was back, as he'd have to bang the door to wake me up. Gingerly I felt around for the doorknob; there was no central button. I felt above it, no chain. I felt along the whole frame, no bolt.

I got back into bed, broken.

There was nothing for it but to wait.

I waited and waited until I couldn't wait any more and eventually fell asleep.

There's a stink, and a stalactite of effluent hangs from the stone barrel ceiling. I'm dressed in nineteenth century clothes and sitting on a stool. Men are in the room, and I'm frightened. Suddenly, Hugo is standing in front of me, holding a bottle in his hand from which he's taking swigs. He's angry, saying I used him, used his money and weren't women all the same, taking what they could, no better than whores? Then his friends gather round.

I awoke with a banging on the door. Or did I dream it? I sat up in bed. 'Who's there?' I said, loudly. Nothing. The rain was coming down harder now and I hadn't closed the curtains. The room was suddenly lit up with silent lightening and I got the shock of my life. In that flash, I'd seen the silhouette of someone by the window, hooded and quite still. Hugo didn't own a hood like that, or at least, I hadn't seen him bring one. Then a clap of thunder came, the loudest so far. 'Hugo? Is that you Hugo?' Lightening blazed again, but this time - no silhouette.

'Who's there?' I felt foolish, but worse still, I felt that calling out made me completely vulnerable. I lay propped up on my elbows for what seemed like half an hour, searching the darkness for anything. But I couldn't keep my eyes open any longer and gave in to sleep.

It starts with a song, someone singing *Mary's Lament.* "*Within a dreary gaol I lie, and none to pity me.*"

Then, as happens in dreams, a knife is put in my hand, a simple, metal kitchen knife, for peeling and paring. Why? I'm defending Hugo's blows. He's teaching me a lesson: it had begun as a punishment. He's wearing a suit with a red silk, polka-dot tie. He tells me to bend over while he shows me what happens to bad girls. Bizarrely, I can smell his breath; it's the smell of rot. His eyes are black, his chin set, his whole being concentrated on the task of bringing pain and effecting obedience. As I struggle, he becomes more rageful and determined. I become conscious of the knife I hold, slowly plunging into meat, hearing the squelch of the stab, then the warmth of the blood oozing over my hand and the look of shock on his face.

Mary appears next to me; her innards have been taken out leaving just a cavity where her stomach should be. 'Have you seen my heart, sweet, bonnie lassie? They've taken my heart.' Her hands are inside herself, searching.

'They took it because you're a murderer,' Hugo says, 'and murderers don't need their hearts when they've been hanged, vile woman.'

'Let him have it,' Mary says, 'Stick him. Stick him.'

I want to stop but I'm tired, I'm frightened. Frightened he'll attack me, and I stab him again and again. It's exhausting, I need to sleep, I need to do nothing. I lie down, but the body of Hugo is rising, he's thumping the door with his head, thump, thump, thump.

I awoke in pain. I'd fallen asleep on my arm, and now I could barely move it. Sunlight streamed through the window.

There was a banging on the door. Was it Hugo?

'Who's there?' I called.

'It's the Police.'

I was confused. Why were the police here? I looked around the room, reminding myself of the nightmare situation I'd found myself in last night, before my actual dreamed nightmare.

'One second.' I sat up and waited for the room to stop spinning. I felt groggy but managed to get to the door and open it.

Before me were two police officers, a man and a woman. It felt so strange. I should have been shocked, but I was calm, and relieved they were here.

'Are you Sophie?' the woman said.

'Yes!' How did they know my name?

'I'm P.C. June Campbell, of Edinburgh City Police.' She held up her I.D. badge. 'You might want to sit down, darlin'?' She put her hand on the light switch. 'Do you mind?' She flicked the switch, and the light came on.

I immediately grabbed my phone and plugged it in. 'Sorry, there was a power cut last night. I've been without comms.' Using the word comms sounded funny, but fitting in the situation, the language the police officers would use.

I sat down, still sleepy.

'Sophie, do you know Hugo Crichton? The man that rented this room?'

'Yes, we rented it together.'

'I'm sorry to tell you Hugo is in hospital. He's been

stabbed.' She squeezed my hand. 'He'll probably be okay, but it's too early to be sure. He was in the pub just across the road.'

'The brothel?'

The other police officer took over. 'Things can get out of hand in these establishments. We think it was the lap dancer. There are four men that saw her do it.'

'Not a woman in a red dress by any chance?'

They looked at each other, then turned back to me silently, and the man gave a tentative nod.

'That'll be the curse.' My words came out without any proper thought. To tell two police officers you suspected that they were investigating a centuries old vendetta would not be helpful. But I wasn't thinking about that, I wasn't thinking at all. That part of my brain was still halfway between my last dream and trying to deal with the irony.

It was the policeman's complete confidence in his truth that riled me into action. 'What makes you think she was a lap dancer?'

'She was wearing stockings and panties for everyone to see.' He frowned in moral disgust. 'We've got her in custody.' He said, in the most matter-of-fact way.

I couldn't help but laugh. But then I was falling, falling back into my dream, and I relished the opportunity to lie down again.

*

'Sophie, darlin'?

The policewoman was standing over me. I'd fainted.

I was struggling to find the right words, my head a hazy mess. 'Hugo could have attacked her first,' I whispered.

'Oh no, he's a law student,' the policeman said.

My phone pinged, and I flicked it on. A photo of the woman in red popped up. It was a message from Airbnb. "Please rate your experience of Jackie's Edinburgh Private Historic Re-enactments – Mary McKinnon."

I chuckled. It was the least appropriate noise, but it made perfect sense, and I passed my phone to the policeman. 'Is this your lap dancer?'

Connie's Blind Love

Epigraph

The Son of Man will send his angels, and they will gather out of his kingdom all causes of sin and all law-breakers, and throw them into the fiery furnace. In that place there will be weeping and gnashing of teeth.

Matthew 13:41-42

Chapter One

The greatest gift is to be born into a kind and loving family. Alistair received something else: a differently wired brain.

His parents struggled to cope with the intensity with which he expressed his needs, for he wasn't like their other two sons, who were happy kicking a football, who would go to bed when they were asked, and who understood that no meant no.

For a while his father was able to come to terms with Alistair's gift, to the degree with which he could monetise it; tasking Alistair, at the age of nine, with the production of bespoke personal computers, often using stolen components, for friends and family who were willing to pay market rates. Then again, when Alistair was eleven, the same client base would pay to have him reprogram their mobile phones to make free calls.

But at twelve Alistair refused to engage in his father's nefarious enterprises and devoted himself instead to his new passion for computer programming. He harnessed his gifts for paying attention to detail, remembering information after hearing it only once, thinking laterally and joining up apparently unrelated facts, and for living and breathing a passion to the point of obsession. The synergy of these talents usually ended in Alistair creating unique and complex solutions for which software houses would reward him generously. Some of Alistair's original coding of sub-routines are still in use today.

But these accomplishments were not understood by his parents, who were frustrated by the way his behaviour impacted their lives. They sought the assistance of CAMHS, the Child and Adolescent Mental Health Service, explaining their son's strange needs for absolute silence and privacy, his mood swings from hyperactivity to mournful depression and his unrelenting obsessions: from the ardent monitoring of weather reports to his collection of clothing labels.

But no further assistance was forthcoming, and they felt that Social Services had merely shrugged their shoulders and sent a few leaflets. They continued to battle it out as best they could.

At seventeen, however, Alistair was awarded Local Authority support for assisted living in the community and was to leave home.

Alistair's reaction to this news was one of relief and excitement. He hoped it would be a fresh start from the run-ins with his disinterested parents, the constant struggle against an overbearing school culture, the episodes with other children's parents and teaching staff he thought oppressively controlling. Even the after-school activities had been a disaster, with him rarely making it past the second week for one reason or other, usually due to some disagreement with the other kids.

A place of his own was what Alistair relished, enabling him to concentrate fully on his new passion for writing code, specifically for the games industry. The only proviso to this utopia was that he needed help with all the annoyances and frustrations that came from the outside world: navigating the world of banks, bills, interactions with neighbours, shopping, choosing clothes, preparing food and keeping warm. For Alistair these challenges seemed harder than rocket science.

It was twenty-year old Constance Ridge—Connie, that was appointed to deliver this personal care. In the beginning her duties were simple: to keep in touch twice a day to make sure that small everyday difficulties were not insurmountable. Often this was only monitoring rather than intervention. That was the Council's policy: to take a light-touch approach and let the client learn progressively, at their own pace.

As the years passed, Connie's involvement was extended as she undertook further studies in advocacy, psychiatry, psychotherapy. There was even a module in occupational therapy.

Connie had many clients, but Alistair was her first and she would say that they grew together, finding their own special way of relating when the everyday difficulties of life flagged up a greater anxiety. For example, Alistair's run-in with a neighbour over noise.

It was Alistair who'd complained. He'd knocked on the neighbour's door and explained his grievance. He did this in a way he thought rational and polite, yet it led to Alistair's first altercation with the police. The neighbour spotted Alistair's special needs and eradicated the problem of a difficult neighbour by insinuating to the police that Alistair had been threatening. Alistair had only been calm and courteous, nevertheless, the confrontation led to Alistair being rehoused to the other side of the estate.

It was this event that spurred Connie into taking the Advocacy course. If she'd been there earlier, she could have helped Alistair avoid what became a very difficult period, for it took a longer time for Alistair, compared to others, to adjust to a new home, and this adjustment was impaired with the distraction of needing to understand what he'd done wrong by his neighbour.

Alistair was lucky to have been assigned Connie as his personal assistant. Many of Connie's colleagues were not so committed to the profession. Some had only chosen it because of a false perception that it was easy and relatively well paid.

When they first met, Connie had come to the door expecting a long amicable discussion, where she could explain what she could provide, and Alistair could detail what he needed. Instead, Alistair had asked Connie to wait in the hallway while he 'just finished off the bit he was doing'. After an hour and a half, Connie called up the stairs to remind Alistair she was still there.

Alistair had been writing the code for a new computer game and as his father put it, he was "unreachable". But having finished his project, the master template for a game's architecture commissioned by Ubisoft, Alistair came downstairs to answer Connie's call. He was in a very good place and decided to celebrate and even communicate with the person who'd come to the door. Maybe they might play a game together.

Connie listened while Alistair described the rules and objectives of his new game. When he asked if she'd like a go, Connie, to Alistair's surprise, agreed and although she was no good at using a controller or indeed picking up the complex interrelated skills and weaponry available to the avatar, she did seem genuinely interested.

After the second hour Connie suggested that she make them both a cup of tea and they could talk about why she'd come. Whist Connie made them a hot drink she did the washing-up and made helpful suggestions for how Alistair could improve the cleanliness and tidiness of the kitchen space and its surfaces.

Alistair asked whether she'd like to go out with him, and so Connie explained that she was with her long-term boyfriend, Euan, who'd she'd met on her sixteenth birthday.

After a few cross-referenced questions, Alistair said, 'So that makes you twenty. That's three years older than me, which wouldn't be outside the confines of social acceptance.'

Connie was going to explain more, as Alistair looked disappointed, but she remembered from her course to avoid oversharing.

Alistair offered that if she ever finished with Euan then she should give him a go, as he'd be able to show her how to use the games console better.

Over the next two years, Connie and Alistair's relationship developed. Connie felt it had achieved a high degree of professional efficacy whilst Alistair would describe their fondness for each other as the best of friends. Alistair learned how to keep his house clean, use his bank account, a lot about personal hygiene, navigating the High Street, about what was appropriate in different situations and how to improve his C.V. But this last lesson was somewhat of a redundant skill, as Alistair was thriving in the video game industry and had made a name for himself.

He would read computer code like most would a novel, laughing at the good bits, irritated at the bad.

Connie learned to adapt her behaviour to avoid giving Alistair mixed messages. He would often check-in to see if she'd "finished with Euan yet".

Alistair's second run-in with the law led to another change of accommodation. In a computer shop, a laptop was being sold for a fraction of its High Street value. But when Alistair tried to buy it, they refused to honour the marked-up price, explaining 'It's a joke, a marketing gimmick that anyone with half a brain would understand.'

Alistair explained what the expressed terms of a contract of law were, and that they had to sell him the computer at the advertised price. The exchange of words became heated, and although Alistair never intended any aggression and most certainly would never have resorted to anything physical, the shop manager called the Police. Alistair tried to explain to them that their line of questioning was against his human rights and quoted a few articles of statute, and so they decided the shopkeeper was correct and arrested Alistair, intending to keep him in a cell until he'd cooled off. Alistair told them, "This is false arrest, and you have no right to detain me".

When Connie collected Alistair from the Police Station, she was shaken and distraught to find that the handcuffs the Police had used had cut into his skin. Also, he'd wet himself, not wanting to ask to use the toilet. In her eyes her "favourite" had been abused through lack of patience and understanding.

Connie's manager felt it was best that Alistair did not live so close to the local Police Station and that a move to a new location would minimise the likelihood of future conflict. Alistair readily agreed, as the suggested new flat had a better internet connection. It was further for Connie to travel but she reassured him that it was no trouble.

Alistair's new apartment was part of a large, vertical estate built in the sixties. The architect had celebrated modern concepts in community interactions and the new brutalist design aesthetic. Alistair didn't mind it; the lift was quick, and his neighbours were quiet. Connie thought it cold and impersonal and didn't like the way there were so many passageways joining from so many directions. The architect had wanted a network, but she wanted Alistair's physical security.

Connie always had the safety of her clients on her mind. Their special needs made them vulnerable to a world that was frenetic, disconnected, judgmental and ultimately tribal. Her clients needed to be assisted through the complexities of expected behaviour and the unwritten laws of interpersonal dynamics. It was too easy for them to be upset by the interactions they had with the people around them, and so easy for them to unwittingly upset others.

She was a born rescuer, which was almost the unwritten requirement in her job description. At school she had helped the victims of bullies, not through her strength but by having the interpersonal skills to reason with the unreasonable. She rescued a supply teacher from a classroom riot, physically leading her out of the room and consoling her. She never hesitated to help the elderly or infirm across the road or help them find their way around the town centre.

This was how she'd met Euan. He'd come to her sixteenth birthday party, a disco at the youth centre, arriving with some of her friends, and Connie and he had danced to the last five songs together. The last, of course, was a slow one and it had been her highlight of the party. But when Euan looked around for his mates, they'd already left, and he didn't know how to get home. Connie got her father to take him. Her father recognised straight away that he was a nice lad and was quite happy for Connie to get involved with a smart, polite and communicative boy.

But Euan grew up, and the boy who couldn't find his way in the world, at least not from a community disco to his home, became the boy who wanted to get lost in the world, and after six years of being with Connie, he announced that he'd joined the Merchant Navy.

Connie asked him to wait and think things through. Maybe they should get married? Maybe she could come too? Maybe she could just wait for him?

Euan did wait, but only long enough for his medical and duplicate exam certificates to come through, and within six weeks he was on his first residential course in Manchester, and shortly after, his first ship.

Connie was in pieces, and the piece of her that gave without question began to question.

*

It was six weeks before Alistair found out that Connie was on her own again. When Alistair complained, 'you're not being much fun', and 'you're not being very chatty', she forgot about oversharing and explained about Euan's unwelcome departure.

Alistair was polite, and initially compassionate, but nevertheless in the end unrelenting. Sometimes he was romantic: 'Euan leaving is a sign that it's our time now'. Sometimes he was passionate: 'I have waited years to kiss your tender lips'. And sometimes he was persuasive: 'We have so much in common Connie, you enjoy being with me and I enjoy being with you. Plus, I really fancy you and I know you fancy me.'

'What makes you say that?'

'For two reasons, firstly, you didn't deny it and secondly, you're always looking at me.'

It was a difficult change for Connie, Euan having been around so much and for so long, and then nothing. It was when she was trying to work out what she'd done wrong that she realised how much she'd ignored Euan. Her parents confirmed it. 'You saw more of Alistair than you did Euan.'

*

It was a day when Alistair was particularly upbeat, having finished a difficult piece of coding, and Connie was particularly lonely. It also happened to be six months to the day that Euan had said he was leaving.

'They're doing a disco at the Community Centre tomorrow.' Alistair said. 'You and I should go together.' This was, he felt, probably his last attempt at what he believed was what should happen: Connie and he moving to the next level.

Connie explained again that it would be inappropriate. She reasoned professionally, calmly and sensitively. Alistair was more direct. 'If you believed that, then you wouldn't be explaining anything, you'd just have said no.'

Connie giggled. Connie weakened. She liked this compulsion of Alistair's, the way he was never overly macho, never resorted to guilting or other covert techniques. He was so different to Euan. They were both attractive, but Alistair was the thinker, maybe not like everyone else, yet wasn't that a good thing? His mind was expansive, thorough, inquisitive, possibly everything Euan wasn't.

Connie knew that the professional fallout from becoming intimate, let alone sleeping with a client, was catastrophic. It was forbidden. That had been in her course notes from the start and had been written up by the course facilitator on the board, to much tittering and childish laughter from the classroom. She had been warned that the forces of time and attention naturally led to attraction and fondness, and it was the duty of the rational professional, the individual most able to master their emotional needs, to quell this tendency and do so proactively. She was the individual in a position of trust and responsibility for a vulnerable person.

Connie's resistance was waning. Alistair had changed over the years, had matured from boy to man. He had taken the skills she'd shared and perfected them. He was still different but all in ways that made her admire him more: his fierce integrity, his passion for creativity and now for his patient charm and romance. Above all, for his unique way of showing love.

Alistair made one last final attempt. The dance was, after all, the very next day. 'If you won't go with me, your best friend, then you should go with a girlfriend. Go out and enjoy yourself, cheer yourself up.'

Connie sensed the end of Alistair's inertia. 'Okay then, why not? But just as friends, yeah? You and I can have some fun, a bit of a boogie.'

That was the preamble, a contract Connie told more to herself, than to Alistair. She'd only been with Euan and now the thought of a love affair with a new boy—man, even if it was someone she'd known for so long and knew everything about, was formidable.

A little of her was frightened it wouldn't work out and that 'going as friends' would be the end of a friendship. A little of her felt that it was time she did something for herself and be as direct as Alistair. She fancied him and part of her was glad Euan had left, glad she had this chance, because Alistair was right, if she was going to go out and have some fun, she'd want to go with a friend and that was him: the eccentric one, not the odd one, the direct one, not the inappropriate one, the rather attractive one, not the quirky one.

The Community Centre was everything it should be. A tiny bar behind slatted bars, a handful of coloured lights not quite illuminating a miniscule stage. Plastic chairs were placed around three walls, giving a space for nervous dancers waiting to be asked. But to Alistair and Connie it was perfect. They were the first to arrive, the first to dance, the first to buy a Coke and an orange juice at the bar, and most importantly, the first to kiss.

Alistair hadn't kissed anyone before, but he'd read about it, and seen it on his screen. He'd seen the films where the girls had complained about bad kissing and committed himself to not disappoint. Connie was not disappointed.

When Alistair had first moved in for a kiss, Connie had led him outside, behind the hall. It was a conscious calculation: all the time their intimacy wasn't witnessed she kept her professional options open.

They were also the first to leave. They'd danced up to the slow songs and then Connie took charge. 'Let's go back to yours.'

Alistair knew from studying films that Connie's words meant she was expecting romance. He was pleased that he'd remembered to put out the coffee cups in readiness, because he knew from those films, when the characters got to the door, one of them would ask 'Are you coming in for coffee?'

Connie was excited. Alistair could dance, whilst Euan had been glued to the plastic chair. Alistair had sipped a Coke; Euan always drank too much. Alistair was happy to leave early and not bother with another pint at last orders. Alistair was a romantic, and even if she was his first, which she knew she would be, she'd be gentle and patient. After all, they had all the time in the world.

Alistair knew that making love was a good thing and would be amazing if you did it with someone you loved. He was very much on top of the world when they'd finished and couldn't wait to ask, 'That was the most incredible thing I've ever done. Does this mean we're going out together?'

'If you would like to, then I would very much like that.'

'Yes, I do want that very much.'

Alistair looked at his radio clock and saw that it was nearly 1 a.m. 'It is getting late though.'

'Would you like to sleep now?'

'Yes, I'm very tired, nicely tired.'

'Did you want me to sleep here too?'

'No, I haven't done that before and I'm a bit worried as I do like to sleep well.'

Connie disguised her disappointment, but as soon as Alistair voiced his wishes, she immediately saw that it would be strange for him. 'That's okay, we can do that when you're feeling up to it.'

'Yes, I think it's something I'd like to try…in the future.'

She giggled. 'I'll see you tomorrow then?'

'Yes, breakfast if you like. I've got sausages in especially.'

'What!' Connie giggled again. 'Did you know I'd come back?'

'No, I just hoped.'

'So did I.'

*

Connie was smiling when she left. She would have preferred to have stayed but it was a feeling of joy that prevailed. It was a new beginning for her, and also an end: she would have to resign on Monday morning and find a way of moving on professionally. Without doubt, she felt being with Alistair was her future, even if that meant upsetting everything in her career.

She waited for the apartment bock's lift, but it seemed lifeless: she would have to face the staircase. First, however, she had to negotiate the maze of interconnecting corridors and walkways to get to it. They were poorly lit, and seemingly with endless blind corners. The first she took slow and wide, but at the second she held her breath and went for it: she wanted to get home. At the third corner her luck ran out.

*

Alistair slept soundly. All his dreams had come true, and he was looking forward to building on a relationship which was already very strong. Three loud knocks at the front door woke him. He thought that strange as there was a doorbell.

Two police officers were at the door, quite a shock for Alistair, standing there in his underpants. His shock turned to alarm when the man and woman appeared angry, and in a hurry.

Initially he was disinclined to answer their questions. He thought of all the statutes he could quote, but the man brought out his handcuffs.

'Are you sure you don't want to answer our questions?'

Alistair complied, explaining his relationship with Connie, telling the story of their night out. 'So, you had sex with Miss Constance Ridge?'

The name sounded strange, and he hesitated. 'I slept with Connie, well we didn't sleep, we made love. Then she went home. Why do you ask? Is Connie alright?'

'We'll ask the questions,' said the man.

'You slept with Miss Ridge and then she went home. At

what time was this?'

'About one.'

'And whose idea was it for her to go home at one o'clock in the morning?' the man asked.

Alistair didn't want to say it was his idea. He didn't want to explain that he liked to sleep alone. This was very personal. Their questions were very intrusive.

'Did you use protection…a condom?' The woman asked.

Alistair's head started to spin, as they hadn't answered his question. 'What's happened to Connie?' he shouted.

'Calm down, son, or we'll have to bring you in,' the man said. 'Answer the officer's question.'

'What question?'

The man, again, dangled the handcuffs.

Alistair remembered his time in the cell, and his sore wrists. He needed help but the person he would normally ask wasn't there. 'Yes, we did.'

'Where is it?

'Where's what?'

'The condom', the woman said.

Alistair thought that the strangest of questions. He was about to laugh, but he saw a picture in his head of Connie saying, "That wouldn't be appropriate". 'It's in the bin.'

As he walked to the kitchen, the police officer's radio crackled. It was a message calling them away. They were gone in minutes, leaving Alistair holding the used condom.

They never told him why they'd come, and their parting words were for him to be available for questioning for the next couple of weeks, if they should want to call again.

The police never did call and neither did Connie. He tried calling her phone, but he only got her voicemail. Alistair worried that he'd been inappropriate and that's why she wasn't returning his calls. But then the overriding fact remained, the Police had come to his door. There must be another explanation.

It wasn't until ten days later that he had a call from Connie's manager, apologising for their lack of communication.

'I'm sure you've seen the local news,'

Alistair was silent. He didn't watch the local news.

'About Constance's death?' he continued.

*

Alistair's bereavement was protracted. The details were too shocking, and no one wanted to communicate them to him. He needed explanations and they weren't forthcoming. Connie's manager only seemed interested in introducing him to Connie's replacement, and Alistair kept on putting that meeting off as it would be an acceptance that Connie wasn't coming back.

Later that month, when he tried to call Connie's manager, he found that he'd been reassigned. His first conversation with the new manager completely dumbfounded him.

'Do you intend taking any legal action against our Department?'

'Why would I do that?'

'Okay, I'll be more candid: Have you sought any legal representation to seek redress for Miss Ridge's behaviour?'

'No, I loved her. Why would I do that?'

Alistair was further confused when the new manager not only didn't answer his question but changed the subject entirely.

There was no one to help him process Connie's death or the predicament he now found himself in. One of the few people he spent time with was never going to be around again.

He tried getting in touch with his parents who he'd not seen in a year, but on the phone they seemed distant and objectionable. When he'd tried explaining about Connie, they responded 'Who, the girl who had her eyes gouged out?'

Alistair hung up, and then Googled Constance Ridge, finding the detail that had been kept from him. Connie had been raped and murdered by someone called The Blinder. The Blinder was a serial killer who had left a trail of misery in the city; nine other women had died from his attacks. Connie was the tenth. His trademark was to put his thumbs in his victims' eyes while saying, "You think you see evil, but now you'll see nothing". This was the chilling report of one survivor, Anne, who ultimately did not survive, taking her own life a year later.

Charlotte had been his first victim, only sixteen, murdered in a graveyard where she was mourning her grandmother's death. Lucy was next, a year later, taken as she cycled back from work.

The police had arrested The Blinder the night Connie and he had gone to the dance, which is why they probably left him in such a hurry.

Alistair found it difficult to process the information and kept on Googling, but he only found more websites confirming Connie's murder. For weeks, he trawled through the internet, exploring other possibilities, because why would someone do that to Connie?

He asked many people, but no one could explain why anyone would do what The Blinder had done.

Connie's replacement was called Simon. He was nice enough and not bad on the games console. In their first meeting, however, Alistair once again became very confused by the conversation.

'Yes, they've appointed me because I'm male, old and married.'

Simon then bellowed with laughter, waiting for Alistair to laugh too, as though Alistair should understand the joke.

'We'll not have any more shenanigans, Alistair. I'm here to help you, not be your friend or friend with benefits.'

Alistair decided it was one of those moments to forget, the product of a mad world.

Simon had never met Connie and either didn't know about her death or didn't want to talk about it. For Alistair there were many months when that's all he wanted to do. Talking about it seemed to give him relief by making it real, to make a space for him to heal. He tried talking with the librarian, the cashier at the corner shop, a couple of online forums, but no one could explain.

The breakthrough came when a lady at the bus stop asked him what was wrong. She listened as Alistair related the sad story.

'What do you think I should do?' Alistair asked.

'You have to move on, love. That's what she'd want you to do. Sometimes there are no explanations for what happens in life. We just have to accept that we've lost something special and move on.'

'Move on?'

'Live for now, darling. Write down your precious memories in a diary, and then continue living life as best you can. That's what she would have wanted: for you to carry on and find happiness as best you can.'

And that's what Alistair did.

Chapter Two

The death of Connie was not the end of Alistair's misery. The investigation into The Binder's other killings, and the news saga following his prosecution and imprisonment, went on for almost two years.

During that time Alistair was chased by journalists for his story. There was a malicious storyline that picked up on Alistair's special needs, and inferred some kind of dereliction of responsibility by him sending Connie home late at night. This was the final straw for Alistair. He moved out of the area to another county. He'd never hit it off with Simon anyway and he decided that Connie had taught him enough to survive. Also, being so successful in his career gave him the confidence to not even tell Social Services where he was going.

It was eight years before Alistair moved on romantically. He did dip his toe in a few times, but he felt online dating needed a subtlety and patience he didn't have and when he did eventually get a date, he was disappointed they weren't like Connie.

They didn't need to look like her, but he wanted the same rapport, a willingness to talk about his projects in game design, the same shared sense of humour, finding the comedy in everyday life. He could say 'bottom' and Connie would giggle. When he told his dry complicated jokes, for example excusing his lack of cooking prowess because he only dealt with kilobytes, she'd give him the benefit of the doubt and laugh anyway.

He could tell when his dates weren't interested. Connie had taught him that when people are bored, they look the other way, or fidget.

There was a woman at work he spent many hours messaging, but when he finally asked her out, she explained she was married. In fact, she'd been married all the time they'd been messaging. She told him she was sorry if he'd felt she was flirting.

He was miserable for a while, but then he remembered what Connie had said: "Disappointments are a way of knowing what you really want, and you can use that to make a plan." That encouraged him to change his dating profile, describing his relationship with Connie, how much he'd loved her and the disaster of her death. He wanted that feeling of being soul mates again, of being in the company of someone who got you, and where you didn't have to explain your jokes or why something was important or interesting.

Almost immediately he got a message. Her name was Sarah, and her profile was almost identical to his, except no one had died. She was looking "for something serious, not a man who only wants one thing".

Their initial and subsequent dates were full of laughter and tender moments. Sarah was amazed and quietly pleased that she was only Alistair's second.

Sarah was a midwife in a general hospital. She liked Alistair's directness, and that he was passionate about what he did for a living, plus he ticked all those other boxes: he had his own teeth and hair and didn't need her money. On the contrary, he was super generous, and she had to insist on paying her way.

Alistair waited to their fourth date to tell her about Connie's murder, which Sarah remembered hearing about on the news. For Sarah, that's when everything fell into place: Alistair's sadness when topics about former boyfriends and girlfriends came up, and his need to know she'd got back home safely. Maybe it was the reason why he thought human nature was strange and difficult to predict. She did ask some questions about Alistair's ordeal, but he became quiet and unforthcoming.

Six months later they found an apartment and moved in together.

One of the synergies of their jobs was that when Sarah worked nights, Alistair would work into the small hours, allowing them to spend time together the next day. There was only one request from Alistair, that when she came back from her nightshift, she didn't wake him up.

They fell into the easy routines of living, working and socialising together. When Sarah went out with her girlfriends, Alistair would stay home and set up an online game with his friends, often testing the projects he'd been working on. He didn't have any friends he could physically go out with, not without Sarah.

Sarah thought this situation should change, and so when the opportunity came along, she arranged it. Her friends were having a Halloween party, and Sarah had to work, so she persuaded Alistair to go on his own.

Alistair wasn't sure about going, but Sarah asked, "What's the worst that can happen?" Alistair could think of quite a few things but knew it was one of those questions you weren't supposed to answer.

He decided that he could always come back early if he got into any trouble, like those confusing situations when people got upset. He knew that people thought he was odd, and he would make allowances for their confused and sometimes hostile reactions. That, he felt, was why he and Sarah got on so well. She had a tolerance, a patience, for his quirks and eccentricities. She might laugh at the way he folded his clothes, lining them up fastidiously and grouping them by colour. But she didn't try and change him. She understood not to wake him when she came home late. He didn't mind if she cuddled up but did nothing more.

He hadn't been to a party on his own for years and remembered they consisted of loud music and lots of people. He planned to find a place on the floor with his bottle of beer and hope the person next to him was friendly. But it turned out to be a much smaller affair.

The host of the party was Sarah's friend, Jacky, whose boyfriend Baz would be there too. Alistair liked Jacky but thought Baz could be a little rude, always making jokes at his expense, jokes that he often didn't understand.

When Alistair knocked on the door, he had one of his panicky worries: would there be one of those weird situations where he didn't know if someone was genuinely interested in what he was talking about or if they were just trying to have sex with him?

Jacky answered the door and made him feel welcome, and he was pleased to find that there were only seven other people there, but then he was on the back foot when he saw the table set for dinner. 'Don't worry about feeding me, Jacky. I've already had my dinner.' But that didn't go down well. He could tell because Jacky pinched her lips to one side and asked if he could try and find room for a little more. He told her, 'Of course', because he knew people liked it when you compromised.

Sitting next to him at the table was Gwyneth, Sarah's friend from college. Alistair hadn't met her before yet took an instant liking to her as she reminded him of someone he'd known at high school, who would talk with him and help get him out of awkward situations. Alistair evaluated that Gwyneth was, however, a bit different: heavier, with longer hair. There were thick clumps of dyed green hair on each side of her head and Alistair tested them by pinching one. 'They're very hard,' he told her.

'They're called dreads. Do you like them?'

'I do have a girlfriend already, but yes, they're kind of fun, like a pair of snakes hanging down.' Alistair realised she didn't like his comment. He could tell, because she didn't show any reaction.

Alistair thought the meal went on a bit, and pondered why people took so long to get through their food. He was offered wine but told them he'd brought beer and put it on the table. Baz poured it into his wine glass and was laughing. Alistair realised that Baz was being funny, probably at his expense, but it didn't matter because, as Connie had told him, he was still the same person, whether Baz liked him or not.

Alistair had met the other guests there before: Peter and Louise, Frances and Gary. He'd quizzed Sarah on how they all knew each other and remembered that Peter knew Baz from work, as they were employed by the same firm of solicitors, but it was only Peter that was fully qualified. Louise had met Peter through Jacky; they'd been to school together and in turn Jacky met Baz through Peter. Frances and Gary lived in the apartment above and had befriended Jacky the day she moved in.

There were three courses to get through and as Alistair had promised, he ate a little bit of each. Jacky nodded her approval. Then Alistair became uncomfortable as the mood changed and everyone got very serious. They took it in turns to talk and spoke more calmly and quietly.

It turned out that they were going to do a séance, because that was what Gwyneth was into. She saw the dead. 'They're around us all the time,' she said, and went on to explain that while they'd been eating there had been two men standing behind them, quietly watching. 'They get lonely and like to be around people.' Also, the gentlemen had been listening to their conversation but there was nothing to be frightened of as they were friendly.

Alistair asked how she knew they were friendly, and she explained that she could tell. He was going to ask her how, but he knew it was rude to ask when a person doesn't know the answer. Then Gwyneth said she was hoping to make a living from seeing dead people, and found a lot of people were interested, especially when she described who was around them. Alistair asked who was around him? But she didn't answer, and Alistair realised she was worried about answering his question. He could tell because she turned the other way and started talking about how she could sell her expertise.

Gwyneth told them that the two gentlemen were not only lonely, but they didn't want to move on to the next place because they weren't ready yet. There was either something they had to do, or something they needed to understand. 'I don't think they're here because of any of us, they probably came with the house. By the way they're dressed, they've been here a long time. Maybe it had something to do with the fire that happened here in the fifties. A whole family perished.'

Alistair thought that was a strange word to use, because it was how you described food that's gone off.

Gwyneth said others would join them soon, 'and in fact, there's a new presence standing behind Alistair.'

Alistair turned to see who it was, and Baz laughed. Alistair didn't mind that Baz had laughed, as it was funny. That's the point: they're not really there.

Alistair turned back around quickly, at the same time as

Gwyneth was reaching out for her wine glass, and they touched hands. In that split second Alistair saw Connie standing opposite him.

Suddenly the dam of nine years of trying not to think of Connie collapsed, and a tsunami of thoughts washed over him. It was impossible for him to process so many thoughts. 'Connie, my love. You're here!'

Sarah had never told her friends about Alistair's murdered girlfriend, anxious that they might one day quiz him about her.

But Gwyneth had seen Connie when she'd walked into the party with Alistair. She did a double take because Connie had her hand through and around Alistair's arm. It was as if Connie were coming as Alistair's girlfriend, but she quickly realised no one else could see Connie. She'd thought better of telling Alistair in such a public forum, but now it seemed appropriate.

'Why is Connie here?' Alistair asked.

Gwyneth was still formulating a calm response when Alistair demanded.

'Why is Connie in Jacky's house?'

Alistair's voice was louder than Gwyneth would have liked.

'She's always with you,' Gwyneth blurted out, immediately annoyed with herself and realising that might be too much information for Alistair. She'd have to finesse these skills, she thought, if she was going to do this professionally.

Alistair squeezed Gwyneth's hand, hard enough to make her wince. Immediately he saw Connie again, this time right next to him.

'Connie!'

She was dressed in the clothes she'd worn to the

community hall disco. She was still beautiful, with the same hair and makeup, but her eyes were wrong. Something had happened to her eyes.

Then Connie held out her hand and stroked his face. 'Careful darling, you're hurting Gwyneth's hand.'

Alistair let go of Gwyneth's hand. 'Sorry,' he said to Gwyneth. But he carried on looking at Connie. He was mesmerised by her. He'd missed her for so long.

Memories of their time together flooded in: the moment she first came to his home, the time she'd come to the police station to help him, their times laughing while playing games, the conversations over coffee, their moments dancing in the kitchen and in the community hall, their moment of passion. A feeling of euphoria swept through him.

Connie's head was now resting on his shoulder and her arm and fingers interlaced with his. His elation grew as he realised that Connie must have missed him too, and that of all the people she could have followed or gone to, she'd chosen him.

Connie hugged Alistair as tightly as she could. 'I'd better go, people don't understand.'

'No!'

But Connie had gone, and Alistair was left staring at the space she'd left. Turning back to the table he saw everyone's faces staring at him. His heart was beating rapidly, and he knew that wasn't good. He had to calm down.

Gwyneth put her hand back on her lap out of Alistair's reach. 'I think it's best if we have a moment on our own. Will you come to the kitchen for a few minutes?'

Alistair followed Gwyneth to the kitchen, leaving the others in silence. She sat him down and poured him a glass of cold water. 'You've had a bit of a shock. Drink this.'

Alistair took a moment to collect himself.

'I haven't seen Connie since she died—well, obviously.'

'It's alright, you don't need to explain.' Gwyneth had already pieced together what had happened from Connie and from what she remembered in the papers. 'I'm so sorry. If I'd known, I'd never have held a séance with you.'

'No, I'm pleased, thank you. I wanted to see her again.'

'But it must be so upsetting.'

'I think I'm more excited. I never got to say goodbye and there was so much I planned to do with Connie.'

'How long were you together?'

Alistair summarised their relationship, begrudgingly including The Blinder in the story. He told Gwyneth of his deep love for Connie and admitted, 'We were only together one night. But I guess I'd loved her for years.'

'Wait a minute,' Baz said, from the doorway. 'I heard this on the news. Didn't the boyfriend send the girl home, on her own, in the middle of the night? That was you, was it?'

'Baz, could you give us a minute?' Gwyneth said.

Alistair looked up, not wanting to think of Baz's judgment of him, but it percolated through, the sadness battling with the euphoria. 'Why did that man do something so horrible?'

Gwyneth tried to think of an answer, but she was speechless; how do you make sense of something so senseless?

'Why was he so evil?' Alistair continued.

'What he did was evil, but it wasn't evil that made him do what he did, it was madness. I meet so many wronged souls and get to find out what motivates their aggressors.

137

It's always some previous trauma that induces madness. A lack of love, mistreatment, suffering of abuse. Mad behaviour causes mad behaviour. No one is born evil.'

'But then I could be mad. I could try and seek revenge.'

Gwyneth put her hand on Alistair's shoulder, but sensing Connie, pulled it away quickly. 'No, you have been looked after. Your soul won't turn. Your heart is true, and you were deeply in love. Connie knows that. It's why she's still here. Keeping you safe and from turning to the madness. She knows you still want her here, and so she stays.

Baz was back in the doorway. 'Can we start the séance now?'

'I'm not sure we should,' Gwyneth said. 'Alistair's had a bit of a shock.'

Alistair immediately thought of the possibility of seeing Connie again. 'I'll be alright.'

'Just give us a few minutes then, Baz.'

'Is she safe?' Alistair said.

Baz tutted sarcastically.

Alistair realised his foolishness; she couldn't be safe, she was dead.

'Shall we do coffee?' Jacky said, as she came through. 'Alistair, if you're okay we'd like to try again, but with somebody different. Is that alright with you, Gwyneth?'

They both nodded, and walked back into the dining room, but Gwyneth couldn't help thinking Alistair would be better off going home.

Peter and Louise didn't look up when Gwyneth and Alistair came back in. Frances and Gary were whispering to each other. Alistair only caught a few words, "What will Sarah do?". Baz was sitting back in his chair, arms crossed and staring intently at Alistair. Alistair avoided eye contact, deciding the room felt more tense than going through airport security.

Gwyneth announced she would prepare the room, and putting her purple carpet bag onto the table, brought out some dark burgundy candles, something that looked like dried plants and a wooden, Eastern figurine. 'I'm just going to cleanse the room from anything harmful.' She lit the end of the dried plants; they were tightly bound together into a long stick-like bunch. 'This is dried sage. Its smoke removes any bad influences lurking in the room. I should have done it when I arrived.' She lit the end of the sage stick which immediately gave a golden flame. Holding the stick up, she cupped her hand behind and blew the flame out with a short precise puff. It continued to smoulder while she took it to each corner of the room, behind the sofa, the curtains and the door, wafting the heady smoke and whispering, 'With this vapour I command the darkness to leave us. Only the peaceful are welcome here.' She lit the candles and placed them in a triangle in the middle of the table.

When Jacky turned off the ceiling light, the room was quite dark, the candles only illuminating their faces and the table.

'Spirts of old, spirts new, join us tonight in this homely space.' Gwyneth's voice was deeper than before, as if she were someone older. 'We honour your presence with our attention and wish to make contact.' Then in her usual voice, 'Could everyone please join hands, and if you can, close your eyes and concentrate on the space around you.'

Suddenly, Alistair felt Baz grab his hand and squeeze it hard, like Simon use to do when they shook hands.

Concentrating was difficult, as all he could think about was Connie and the way she'd held him. The smell of her perfume had been exactly the same as when she was alive. Then he felt Gwyneth gently feel for his hand, which he welcomed, hoping to see Connie again. He opened his eyes and searched the room.

'Alistair, please focus your attention,' Gwyneth said. She called out to the room with the same words as before, this time finishing with a soft melodic hum. She gently tapped the tabletop three times. 'We enter as you enter. Show us your light.' She returned to quiet tuneful humming. After a couple of minutes Gwyneth spoke once more. 'Is there anyone in our circle that would like to talk with someone who has passed?'

It was Baz who spoke. 'Jacky and I would like to ask Constance what her intentions are. Why did she come tonight?'

'We are not here to interrogate Connie,' Gwyneth said. 'Connie is here for Alistair; that's all we need to know.'

Gwyneth called to the room again, but the minutes passed without event. Then there was a sharp whine of wind down the chimney, and she felt a change in the room's mood. There was a new presence, and she opened her eyes. The two old men were still there, sitting on the sofa. Connie was standing behind Alistair with her hands on his shoulders. But there was something else, something she couldn't see. 'Who's there? Show yourself!' With growing certainty she felt the séance should not continue.

The new presence remained hidden, but Gwynneth heard a quiet, sarcastic laugh. Only she felt and heard it, and something in her stomach told her that it was not a good spirit. This had happened to her before, it wasn't uncommon. You called out to all spirits and never knew who would answer. However well you cleansed the room it was possible to attract a malevolent or unhappy spirit.

She felt it growing in power and sensed it was something old that moved like a shadow. It was to her right and low to the ground, creeping nearer to her, or perhaps towards Alistair. Then she realised, with a shock, that the spirt was attracted to Connie. She knew that bad spirits often misbehave in the Waiting Room, continuing to behave as they did when they were alive. Was this new presence attracted to Connie's goodness, wanting to unsettle her? To this presence, Connie's beautiful light was like blood in the ocean to a hungry shark.

Gwyneth broke the circle, releasing Alistair's and Peter's hands. Instinctively, everyone else released their grip too.

'Sorry everyone, but I think all my energy might have been used up connecting with Connie.'

Ending the séance was the only way she could think of to protect Connie. She hoped that without the attention and focus of the group, the energy of the spiritual space they'd created would diffuse.

Alistair wasted no time in supporting Gwyneth. 'You definitely have a talent, Gwyneth. Maybe other people are disappointed not to have spoken with someone they love, but I'm certainly not. Not with the moment I had. It's incredible to be in contact again with the love of your life.'

Alistair noticed that the others suddenly became serious again. Jacky looked worried and Baz angry. Alistair could tell because his face was like a screwed-up hanky. Only Gwyneth was smiling, but it wasn't a happy smile. She suggested that maybe it was better if he went home.

Alistair knew that when people said this, he shouldn't work out why. It was better to leave straight away.

Gwyneth hoped that Connie would follow Alistair home and in doing so, move away from the unwelcome presence.

Alistair thanked everyone for helping him get in contact with Connie. He shook everyone's hand, just like Connie had taught him to do, and soon he was on his way home.

Whilst getting ready for bed, he thought of the funny ending to the evening, putting it down to being too tired. Sure enough, it wasn't long before he was fast asleep.

Somewhere in the middle of the night, Alistair felt Sarah reach over and pull him in close. Her hand was cold, and although she was very gentle, it was a bit more of a squeeze than usual, as though she were trying to persuade him to wake up. But he knew if he just ignored her, she'd give up and go to sleep. Alistair managed not to come round completely and soon dozed off again.

Sometime later he heard the front door open. She can't have closed it properly, he thought. He felt Sarah lift her arm. Good, he thought, she was going to sort it out.

He heard her go to the loo and fiddle with her clothes. Then she got back into bed and snuggled up to him once again. Alistair thought that strange, as they didn't usually have two cuddles, but at least she'd warmed up.

'Sarah! We've already had our cuddle.'

'Yeah, but not since this morning.'

'Not since half an hour ago.'

'What are you talking about? I've just got home.'

Sensing something was wrong, Alistair opened his eyes. There in front of him, sitting on the wing-backed chair by the window, was Connie, looking at him with her funny new eyes. He couldn't fully understand her expression, but she seemed calm and content.

Sarah tugged on his shoulder, 'Alistair, what do you mean?'

'Oh, yeah sorry—don't know—ignore me. Night

Sarah.'

 Connie smiled and mouthed 'Good night'.
 In the morning she'd gone.

Chapter Three

The morning after the séance, Gwyneth called Sarah to make sure Alistair was alright. She was careful not to divulge too much about the evening, merely reporting that Connie's spirit had visited them and although Alistair was initially shocked, he'd come to terms with it by the end of the evening and seemed grateful that she'd made an appearance.

After their phone call, Sarah immediately called Jacky. Baz was listening in the background, and they were not so reserved as Gwyneth, warning Sarah that Alistair seemed very excited that his old love had sought him out. Sarah, however, did not feel threatened and was only worried about the impact on Alistair's emotional peace. After all, it had been many years since he'd been reminded of the event that brought him so much anger and sadness, the darkest period of his life. Connie's visitation risked immersing him back there once again.

Sarah carried on as if nothing had happened, and she soon forgot about Connie's reappearance. For Alistair, life appeared to carry on as normal too, with one significant exception: he continued to spend time with Connie.

He had no control over when she came; it was always a time of her choosing. It wasn't every night. Some weeks she didn't come at all, and others she came every night, but always when Sarah wasn't there, and most often when Alistair had had a bad day.

Often Alistair would wake up and find that Connie was wrapped in his arms, or she would be spooning him from behind. He'd have to spend a few moments working out whether it was Sarah or Connie. Connie's scent was the giveaway: the blueberry scented shampoo that she'd used. Usually they would talk briefly, and he would fall back to sleep, but sometimes they'd have long conversations. Alistair would tell Connie what was troubling him, what was unfair, what was weird, why the world didn't make sense, or how he found it difficult to understand why people did what they did. He also told her the good news, how he'd received acclaim from work colleagues or about the success of the games he'd worked on. He didn't tell her how happy he was with Sarah, how she made him feel protected and more connected with the world. It didn't seem appropriate to talk about her.

There was one awkward moment when Sarah returned from a nightshift, and in a sleepy state he'd called her Connie. Fortunately, Alistair realised his mistake and pretended to be talking in his sleep, which was kind of true. Either way, it meant he didn't have to explain himself.

He never considered this reconnection with Connie as cheating or even something disloyal. It felt natural, and he couldn't see how it was doing Sarah any harm. He didn't feel the need to explain anything to Sarah and hoped it would continue. He never asked himself whether Connie was fulfilling something missing in his life. For him it was purely healing from the past. In fact, it was a chance to join up the past with the present. Now, no time was wasted wondering if Connie was happy, and it was reassuring to know she wasn't suffering. He was relieved to know that she wasn't angry with him for not walking her home, because if that was the case she would have said so. Alistair was able to fully concentrate on his work for the first time in years, knowing that everything in his life was as it should be, balanced, in harmony, and without tension.

*

Six months after the séance, Gwyneth's new career was taking off and her life was further blessed with a new boyfriend, Greg. Sarah noticed Gwyneth mention him in a Facebook post, and invited them both round, as a way of getting to know Greg. Subconsciously, she also wanted to check him out. Was he good enough for her girlfriend?

The evening had been fun. They had finished their three-course meal and were chatting over coffee when Gwyneth sensed Connie. She didn't tell the others, because it wasn't that kind of evening, and if anything, she felt she owed it to everyone not to talk about her new career in contacting the spirit world. The evening was about getting to know each other, not her boasting about how well it was going for her.

She noticed that Connie's presence grew stronger, her light shining brighter. For the most part she was sitting still on the sideboard, swinging her legs and watching the meal, with Alistair unaware she was there. Then Connie's disposition changed; her light grew purple, and the edges of her appearance blurred. She walked over to Greg and stood behind him, pretending to lift a mask from his face. As she did this, Greg's face turned red. His expression looked sinister, angry and although his smile was normally friendly and charming, it now appeared ugly, a thin sneer distorting his face. Connie faded away while looking directly at Gwyneth.

'Isn't that right Gwynnie?' Greg said.

Gwyneth had been so distracted by Connie's actions she'd missed the conversation. 'Sorry, what is?'

'I'm the best plumber in town,' Greg said, laughing.

'For an electrician, you're amazing.'

'Can I borrow you then?' Sarah said. 'Just for a tick, I promise. I just want to know if it's been properly fitted. I've had boilers before, and this looks wrong.'

'Sure, no problem. Take me to your boiler.'

Greg followed Sarah out of the room and Gwyneth grabbed her opportunity. 'So, Alistair, how has it been going since the séance?'

Alistair tried to understand the real question. "How's it been going", often meant different things. He wondered if she was on to him 'Oh you know, ups and downs, mostly up. Work is fantastic.'

'You're still seeing Connie, aren't you?'

Alistair again tried to work out where Gwyneth's line of enquiry was going.

He nodded. 'Yes, it's okay. We're just keeping in touch.'

'Is that a euphemism?'

Alistair fiddled with his napkin, struggling with the idea of being involved in a euphemism, 'No, really we just talk.'

'About what?'

'Well, that's the funny thing. We talk about what we used to talk about. I try and tell her about what's going on now, but she doesn't pass comment, or tell me what's she's doing, or what she feels about The Blinder. Actually, nothing about anything that happened after she died.'

'Is that surprising?'

Alistair pondered and looked stumped.

'You only have the past, Alistair. You can't have a future with Connie.'

Alistair remained silent. Part of him wanted to argue and prove her wrong, but he suspected she was right.

'Connie's a rescuer, isn't she?' Gwyneth continued.

'She certainly is—the best.'

'You know she's here to protect you? When people suffer, it sometimes comes out as anger. They focus on their sadness, seek revenge and try and take back control in ways that grow ever increasingly like the meanness that was used against them. Connie's here to stop that happening.'

'She doesn't need to do that. I'm never really that angry anymore, not after meeting Sarah. But I did want to understand, you know, why it happened. And know that Connie is alright now.'

They could hear Sarah and Greg returning.

Gwyneth squeezed Alistair's hand. 'If you ever need to talk about it, call me.'

Alistair nodded.

When they came back, Sarah had an expression that Gwyneth couldn't read, and when their eyes met, Sarah raised her eyebrows.

The next day Gwyneth called Sarah to thank her for the meal and then asked what she really wanted to know. 'Sorry to ask, but why the face, when you came back into the room with Greg?'

'I'm not sure I should say.'

'Go on.'

'It was just something he said, that was a little—very weird. "I can come back on my own if you like, when Alistair's not in".'

'Oh!'

'Yeah, maybe he'd had too much to drink.'

But it wasn't the drink, and it wasn't a one off, and Gwyneth soon got a chance to piece together the real Greg, who liked to sleep around. Connie had tried to rescue her and sent a very deliberate and accurate message. Gwyneth decided Connie was a special kind of spirit, sensitive and active, but she couldn't decide whether that was good for Alistair, or, for that matter, Sarah.

*

A few weeks after breaking up with Greg, Gwyneth was sitting in her kitchen contemplating the apparition of Connie revealing Greg's true nature. She decided to Google "Connie" and more specifically "The Blinder", hoping to put her mind at ease. She received a shock.

Only yesterday, The Blinder had taken his own life in prison. All the major news sites covered the story, a couple with a complete summary of his murderous past, naming the victims and detailing his atrocities. The Guardian pointed out that it was the anniversary of his mother's death and so too, the exact same date of four of his murders. There was a picture of Connie and a quotation from the court case, that he'd regretted "killing her so quickly, not having had much time to play".

The Blinder had pleaded not guilty, not because he hoped to be acquitted, but because he'd enjoy a trial that would allow him to relive all his misdeeds. Also, when he'd described his killing methods and his hatred for women, he'd enjoyed seeing the pain and anguish amongst the faces in the court room.

At the reading of his sentence, the judge had described him as a monster. The Blinder had merely smiled and signalled his agreement.

Gwyneth felt a piercing pain in her head, like a migraine but more localised. It grew in intensity and then faded, leaving her with a memory of the dark presence she'd felt during the séance at Jacky's house, the same night Connie had appeared. It can't have been The Blinder, she thought; the seance was months before his death. But she knew instinctively that the presences were related.

While sipping a fortifying gin and tonic, she calculated the consequences of The Blinder's death. Connie was potentially in danger and Gwyneth was in a position to help her. If events unravelled the way she suspected, Alistair too could be saved from being traumatised all over again.

Gwyneth picked up her phone. It was 4pm, she had just enough time. She pressed the telephone icon. 'Sarah, it's urgent, can I meet you right away? Somewhere near your home?'

'Sure, but why not meet me at home?'

'No, it's something Alistair can't hear, not straight away.'

Gwyneth hurriedly packed her purple bag. She'd need most of her tools and equipment, for she knew anything might happen.

They met at the pub at the end of Sarah's road. Fortunately, it was busy, allowing their whispers to be drowned out by the background noise.

'I might celebrate this spontaneous meeting with a glass of wine,' Sarah said.

'Please don't. If you agree to help me, you'll need a level head.'

Sarah looked alarmed.

'Is Alistair at home?'

'Yes.'

'Good, then listen up because if we do this thing, we'll hopefully be starting within the hour and even then, it's cutting it fine.'

'What on earth is going on?'

Gwyneth related the news of The Blinder's suicide, and

of how his spirit would be connected with Connie's.

'Sarah, I need to tell you something that you might find difficult. Alistair has been seeing Connie and they've been spending time together.'

In shock, Sarah laughed, and then looked confused. 'Since the séance? How long have you known?'

'From when we came for that meal.'

'Why didn't you say anything?'

'Because it's not my place to interfere.'

'But it is now?'

'Trust me, I'm thinking of the best for Alistair. He's my client, so to speak. They're not having a love affair. Connie came back to protect Alistair, to protect his spirit, to keep it light and true, to keep away the bitterness, sadness and anger that comes from being different in this intolerant world and having suffered such a devastating loss. She came back to help him through.'

Sarah looked away; she didn't know what to do with the information. 'Surely, this is good news. It means Alistair doesn't have to worry about bumping into The Blinder or even hear that he's been given parole.'

'No, the danger is The Blinder will now enter the Waiting Room, and he'll probably come looking for Connie.'

'The Waiting Room?'

'The place where spirits get stuck between this life and the next part of their journey.'

Sarah sighed. 'But surely she can't come to any harm? She's dead.'

'If The Blinder gets to Connie, there's no knowing what he'll do. Connie may become stuck in the Waiting Room, keeping her from moving on to the good place or, worse still, he may hold her there in perpetuity, brutalising her.

That's how he got his kicks in this world, so it's how he'll behave in the Waiting Room. She might not have enough resilience to find Alistair for years, by which time she'll be a different spirit, damaged, broken, maybe even hostile.'

'To Alistair?'

'Possibly.'

Sarah drew breath. 'Okay, what do we do next?'

'Persuade Alistair to give her up. Let her move on to the next place out of the Waiting Room and away from The Blinder. And we need to do it now. Literally every moment counts.

'Won't Alistair just think I'm jealous? Wouldn't it be better coming from you?'

'No, we can't explain that The Blinder is a threat. Alistair might tell Connie and then she may hide away in a panic. He needs to persuade her to transcend— for her own good.'

*

When Sarah and Gwyneth opened the door they found Alistair dancing to the radio. He stopped when he saw their faces. 'What's up?'

Sarah turned off the radio. 'Alistair, I need to talk to you in the bedroom.'

Gwyneth started to unpack her carpet bag. 'Good luck, you two. I'll be right here if you need me.'

In the bedroom, Sarah got Alistair to sit on the bed. 'Gwyneth told me about you seeing Connie.'

Alistair froze; suddenly the niggle of doubt that his relationship with Connie was inappropriate crystalised into guilt. 'Oh, yes, but it's not what you think.'

'I know what it is, and I think it's wonderful that Connie

continues to support you. It must have been awful to have lost her that way. I'm not here to scold you. I'm here to save something that is beautiful. Love is always beautiful.'

Alistair relaxed his shoulders. 'But?'

'But I think it's time now for Connie to move on. There's a place in heaven for her, where she belongs, and she'll be safer.'

'Safer?' Alistair looked out the window. The sun was split in half as it dropped below the opposite apartment block.

Sarah squeezed Alistair's hand. 'Because that's what you're supposed to do after you die. You're not supposed to hang around in this world.'

Alistair turned away from the sunset and from Sarah, contemplating letting go of Connie. It had been wonderful having her around, having the time to say goodbye. Isn't that what they'd really been doing?

Sarah cleared her throat, running out of ideas, feeling guilty for pressuring Alistair. 'Maybe I'm not being fair.'

'No, you're right. I've been holding on to her and that's what's not fair. And anyway, I've got you.'

Sarah sat on the bed and held Alistair's hand. 'Not that it's the same, but yes, I'm here to love you.'

'And I'm here to love you.'

'Are you ready then?'

Alistair nodded.

'Gwyneth gave me this talisman, to give to you.' Sarah held a tiny doll in the palm of her hand, made from ebony and about two inches tall. 'When you hold it, you'll see Connie. You won't need to wait for her to come.'

Alistair stood up and walked to the window.

Sarah realised she had more to do, time was running out. This could all go pear shaped very quickly, yet she had to keep the urgency out of her voice, 'So, you can call her now, if you want. Would you like me to be with you or do you want some privacy?'

'No, stay. I've no secrets from you.'

Alistair walked back and sat down. Taking a deep breath, he took the talisman and closed his eyes. When he opened them, Connie was there.

He looked away, suddenly mindful of his lack of preparation, fearful that he might upset her, sad that his act of love may be misconstrued as a lack of love. 'Connie, my love, I've got something to say.'

He stopped. There was something about Connie that was different. It took a few moments for her to lose her transparency, and although she now seemed solid, she had another kind of ethereal quality. He realised there was a shimmer of gold to her skin, and she was much taller than before.

She smiled at him and turned sideways. He was astonished to see a pair of wings stretching her full height. The feathers were iridescent gold, sapphire and rose. He could not have imagined her more beautiful, yet here she was, a heavenly vision.

'I have been chosen as an angel to do God's work,' Connie said in a deep, unfamiliar voice. 'I must go now to do my first duty. Do not watch, as it may be quite brutal. I must avenge an injustice to my sisters.'

Alistair knew Connie didn't have any sisters but didn't disagree.

'Let me introduce you to my sisters.'

The back of the bedroom wall was rapidly becoming translucent and slowly nine other angels appeared. They too had the most incredible richly coloured and luminescent wings. One angel had purple and green feathers, another the hues of the forest. They stood serenely, yet their presence was powerful and ordered.

'Goodbye then, my darling,' Connie said, from further away. 'Thank you for your love. You will not see me again, but I know you will be safe with Sarah. I am going to avenge the torture and death of my sisters. The Blinder will be bleached from this realm and every other.'

In an instant Connie and the angels dissolved, replaced with the hard reality of the bedroom wall.

Alistair had never seen Sarah look so terrified.

He stood up. 'Connie's in danger. We've got to tell Gwyneth.'

*

Gwyneth sat on the sofa with her spiritual weaponry and shields. She had prepared herself to go into the spirit world and distract The Blinder, giving Alistair time to let Connie go. Her strategy was dangerous; she would be the vulnerable woman, meek and mild, willing to help all: The Blinder's favourite target. She'd never entered the Waiting Room before with the deliberate intention of confronting an evil entity. In her circle it was expressly frowned upon for there were dangers with unknown risks. Could her physicality be threatened? Would the experience lead to trauma?

Gwyneth rapped three times on the coffee table and said the incantation aloud. 'Veil that is hidden, gate which stands ajar, loosen thy chain and break thy lock, show me The Blinder awaiting his hell.'

Entering the Waiting Room, she found a dimly lit space. It was difficult to make anything out, but as her eyes adjusted, she recognised it from the press coverage of

Connie's death. She was in a brick-lined passageway with a concrete floor and no doorway in sight. The air was damp and stagnant and all she could hear was the sound of dripping water falling into a puddle.

She didn't have to wait long.

A rough hand seized her from behind, pulling her neck back hard. Another grabbed her around her chest, trapping her arms and lifting her off her feet. Although shaking with fear, Gwyneth was prepared, and clenching her phial of holy water, she squeezed and shattered it. Instantly The Blinder released his grip with a hiss.

'Ah, you have tricks, little witch.'

'Enough for you, little coward.' She stepped back and looked at him. He was actually quite short compared to the man she expected. But it was the angry red scar that connected his mouth with his right ear, that made him difficult to look at.

'Preying on the weak. You're just a common playground bully.'

'What a lovely scene: little children being killed.' He stepped closer to her, looking vulnerable for a moment. 'Wait-.' The Blinder sniffed the air. 'You're hiding something from me.' He pushed Gwyneth backwards. 'Connie! You've got her here.'

The Blinder's mocking laughter filled the passageway. 'Excellent, I will have her again. Our last encounter finished far too quickly. But for now, you will do.' He seized Gwyneth's throat with both hands. 'Take a last look with your ugly eyes. You think you see evil, but now you'll see nothing.' He brought his thumbs up over her eyes, enjoying the fear he saw in them. But before he could pierce their soft jelly with his dirty nails, Gwyneth vanished, and he was left holding nothing.

The passageway was gone, and in its place shone a brilliant, shimmering light, not unlike the sunrise. Emerging from the centre of the light, Connie stepped forward with Gwyneth in her arms, much as a parent would carry their child. Putting her down, they stood next to each other. The Blinder noticed how Connie stood at least two feet taller than Gwyneth.

'We have been waiting for you,' Connie said, her voice quiet in the now open space.

Spreading her wings, the nine other angels appeared beside her.

The Blinder was silent for a moment, but without sufficient imagination or foresight to be frightened said, 'You've brought the other whores then?' He looked closely at his victims, feeling a sense of accomplishment. 'Charlotte, nice wings. They'll look great wrapped around your neck.' He turned to Lucy, standing at the end. 'I enjoyed your death the most. A lot of blood, as I remember. I wonder if you still bleed?'

'We are here to cleanse the world of your foul presence,' Lucy said.

'There is no place in God's creation for your evil,' Connie said.

Sarah and Alistair's lounge suddenly appeared. Alistair and Sarah were sitting on the sofa and Gwyneth walked over to sit between them, placing a protective arm around each of them.

'You've brought a little audience with you,' The Blinder jeered.

'It's right that the world should witness your end,' Charlotte said.

'You can't end me; I'm already ended.' He laughed like a madman.

157

'You will now learn the original meaning of the word decimate,' Connie said. 'Each of us will take a part of you, as you took from us. We will travel our separate ways and dispose of your body; you will not be complete and therefore cannot transcend in any form. You will no longer be. Not even in hell.'

The room solidified and expanded, encompassing the angels and enveloping The Blinder, as the walls grew to twice their height. There was no ceiling above them, only the night sky.

One by one, each of the spotlights exploded. The HI-FI burst into action, playing a loud cacophony of random songs. With a violent crack the mirror on the wall behind the sofa shattered into large pieces, one piece crashing to the floor. Finally, the picture above the fireplace slid to one side, smashing and splintering onto the mantelpiece.

Connie's wings unfurled even further, as she too seemed to grow in size, rising higher into the air. 'Sisters, take what is yours and bury it far away.'

Charlotte, unarmed, walked slowly towards The Blinder.

'You can try, you dumb bed warmers,' The Blinder bellowed.

As she drew closer, The Blinder looked small and insignificant compared to Charlotte's mighty wings. Lifting her left wing, she swept it across him. Shocked, The Blinder gave no resistance.

'I will take his neck,' Charlotte said, 'and then we don't have to hear his nonsense.' Holding her piece of The Blinder, she flew off far above them, disappearing into the dark sky.

Lucy was next to continue his disfiguration, calmly flying towards The Blinder and drawing a wing across his body. 'I will take his penis, because that is what he will miss the most.' She then flew out of the window.

One by one the angels tore into The Blinder, and he grew smaller and smaller until only his silent head remained. His eyes rolled comically from side to side, and his mouth opened but no sound emerged.

Connie bent down and picked up The Blinder's head like a tenpin bowling ball, a finger in each eye, a thumb in his nose, then casually dropped it into the fireplace. On contact with the metal grate his head burst into flames.

Walking to the sofa, Connie sat next to Alistair. The four of them watched as The Blinder's head burned and melted away. The small part of God's universe that had been plagued by The Blinder for so long, was finally freed.

Connie sighed contentedly. 'It's time for me to go now. Thank you all, for your help. I trust you will look after each other.' With a kiss to Alistair's forehead, Connie became translucent.

Alistair reached out for her, but his hand passed straight through, and moments later she'd transcended.

*

Witnessing the rise of the angels and the demise of The Blinder had been exhausting, and Alistair and Sarah were asleep in each other's arms within the hour.

The next day Alistair was quiet, almost non communicative, and he decided to have a day off.

Sarah waited for Alistair to speak about what they'd seen, feeling it wasn't her place to talk about Connie.

She watched him as he went through the torment of finally losing her and recognised the signs of him sinking into his internal world.

It wasn't until five days later that Alistair finally told Sarah what he felt, as he held her hand on the sofa.

'Connie will make the best angel. She was born to help people. Plus, it's like she's having her life now, isn't it? Her life was cut short, but this will make up for it.'

It was Sarah's turn to be quiet. She let Alistair's words linger, and be celebrated with silence, as they both remembered Connie: brave and powerful, righting a monstrous injustice.

'She was tall though, wasn't she?' Alistair said, smiling.

'She was a giant. Tell me she wasn't that tall when you went out with her?' Sarah laughed.

'She wouldn't have got through the front door! And wasn't she an angel with attitude?'

'What, burning his head? Hey, you should put her in one of your games.'

And that was the spark for an idea with which Alistair immortalised his love, in a game he called *Sisters Without Mercy*.

Deauville du Coup

Epigraph

Assumptions are the termites of relationships.

Henry Winkler

Chapter One

I was on my way to Deauville du Coup, one of my favourites of Lutyens's houses. Ironically, however, Sir Edwin Lutyens never put his name to the design. The client fell out with the both the builder and architect before the house was halfway completed. This may explain why the house has such an ill-suited name for a home in the village of Bemblebury, Surrey. The first owners never actually lived there. They flipped it before it was finished, hoping to profit from the provenance, dubious as it was, of one of England's finest Arts and Crafts architects. It was them that christened the house with its pompous name, although they weren't even French; they just liked the sound of it.

Nevertheless, it is a house that has come to define so much of me, including why I chose to study architecture. I only managed two years of the seven—it was difficult, but that led me to becoming an interior designer, a career that I have excelled in. *Elisabeth Riley Interiors,* that's me, patronised by the Duke and Duchess of Kent. Most of all, it was the house that gave me the first clue that I was gay. Curious, then, that I have never been in the building, but that was all going to change in the next hour; my childhood dream was about to come true.

Bemblebury is a one church, one school, one shop village, surrounded by large manor farms and forested woodland. The posh part was built in the twenties, its large houses endowed with grand gardens. The cheap estate was built fifty years later with what we now call affordable housing. This is where my parents bought, and where I grew up. They chose the last plot, the one that no sensible person would buy, but it was all my mum and dad could afford. The house was built on the site of a disused railway and would probably suffer from subsidence—it did.

However, our home had great access to a little used public footpath. Our back gate literally opened onto it. This allowed me to take a shortcut to school and then later a quicker way to the bus stop for secondary school. It meant going through the posh side of town. The residents didn't like me walking through their territory, and I was silently admonished with lots of annoyed faces. You'd think that would teach me to hate them, but instead, it taught me to respect them and want to elevate myself to their station.

One of the grand houses I passed was Deauville du Coup, with its topiary garden, castellated hedge, manicured lawns, the ridiculously tall chimneys, steep roofs, beautiful symmetry and elegant walls. It was everything our seventies box wasn't.

Nine times out of ten, when I passed, there would be a boy in the window, reading. This boy, George, used to go to my primary school. I could remember him well. He was quiet, with an ironed shirt, bespectacled and prone to wet himself. Well, it probably only happened the once, but of course the other boys never forgot and took every opportunity to remind him.

This window seat of George's became the focus of my dream world, my fantasy of how things should be when I grew up. I too wanted a reading seat in a window overlooking a beautiful garden.

Now, very soon, I was to step inside this seed of my decades-long fantasy. My route to Deauville du Coup this evening was through the woods, a short stretch from my new home in the cheap end of the posh part of Bemblebury. Indeed, that was why we, my wife Mary and I, had received our invitation.

George's parents, who I'd never met, had learned through the residents' association that we'd moved in, and we were being welcomed at one of their regular cocktail parties. I knew they were regular as the invitation had said "It's that time again, another Goldsmith bash".

Their surname didn't ring any bells, but then why should it? George hadn't stayed at school past the first year and I'd never got to know him. It was public knowledge that his anxiety had got the better of him, the bullies had won, and George was home-schooled instead. I wondered, given the amount of time he spent reading, whether he'd actually schooled himself. It was such a waste when they lost him in a tragic accident twelve years later. Who knows what kind of man he would have become?

Mary was surprised that I was willing to arrive at the party on my own. I'm not particularly introverted but, let's face it, arriving as a couple is much less intimidating. Usually either one of you has the face or the right words to break the ice with the hosts. But I knew Mary wouldn't get there until late and I didn't want to miss anything. After all, I couldn't be sure we'd be invited again. I wanted as much time in the house of my dreams as I could get.

It was good to have left the darkness of the woods and to see before me the object of my desire, in all its glory, set in the serenity of a full moon and framed by the verdant Surrey hills. Shortly, I rang the bell.

The door was opened by a smart, barrel-shaped man, moustached and greying, but with a smile that promised a cheery disposition.

'Elisabeth, I presume. Donald Goldsmith, wonderful to meet you at last.'

He held his hand out for me to shake. He clasped my hand and didn't let go until we were over the threshold and standing in the hallway. It felt reassuring, welcoming.

'Now, what can I get you? How about a gin? That'll set you up for all the people that want to meet you.'

The hallway was wide and long, as I would expect for such a grand exterior. This was a hallway designed to impress and it had been thoughtfully presented. They hadn't settled for dreary reproduction mixed with the odd antique highlight, or bland whitewashed walls. No, they had taste. I felt relieved; these owners deserved to be here, and my dream had been looked after. Tall ceilings were framed with deep plaster cornicing, full drop curtains, bold colours mixed with sympathetic patterns, contemporary furniture spiced with retro highlights. Everywhere I looked gave me an excited feeling that the house had been celebrated. The Goldsmiths may have chosen the house for its prestigious architect, but that was only a seedbed for their creation. Money alone could not have created this look; this was born from love and attention, a true passion for interior design.

Donald led me through the house: a subtly lit drawing room, a snug study and a rear hallway filled with gorgeous plants and life size statues. Every room was filled with guests. He took the long way around to the kitchen while speaking of his love for Bemblebury, his wife's active role in the W.I., the residents' association, his woeful commute and his hopes for retirement.

The kitchen was another success, avoiding a dreary parody of a stately home museum exhibit. It was an exquisitely displayed mix of hyper-modernism and intimate country house, a difficult look to pull off.

'And this is my wife, Hilary,' Donald said, looking at her as he put his hand softly on my shoulder. 'Hilary, our new neighbour, Elisabeth.'

Hilary held out her hand, 'I've heard so much about you and, of course, *Elisabeth Riley Interiors.*'

Hilary Goldsmith was glamourous, with a warm smile. If Donald was an old pair of slippers, she was fresh out of the box Manolo Blahniks.

I was captivated. She was a little old for me, but, wow, I hoped that I looked as good as her when I got to that age. Her emerald cocktail jacket glittered with sequins. Her immaculately cut shoulder length bob was coloured a sophisticated grey. Even sitting on a bar stool, she held herself like a regal statue.

'And it's Elisabeth with an 's', isn't it? I've read some of your articles in *Homes and Gardens.* You write well, especially your home histories.'

'Thank you, and I must compliment you. I absolutely love what you've done with Deauville du Coup. I knew it would be impressive, but you've excelled.'

I'd gushed, while Hilary was more moderated. 'Why, thank you. But I thought you were new to Bemblebury?'

'No, I grew up here.' I hoped so much she wouldn't ask where, because I'd have to disclose my paltry beginnings. 'I passed your house every day, on my way to school.'

Hilary's composure took a knock. 'Oh! I see.'

I took a gulp of my gin, hoping for inspiration. I wanted Hilary back in the comfortable zone, so I explained. 'I knew George, when he was at school, obviously.' This wasn't working, her smile had gone completely. I grabbed for something positive. 'And you have a beautiful daughter, don't you?' I remembered her as well as George sitting in the window seat. 'Is she here—tonight?' Now I felt like a stalker.

Hilary didn't say anything and looked straight past me. I guess I'd assumed that, because George's death was decades ago, it was safe to mention his name. But no, I'd dug a hole for myself and crawling out wasn't happening.

As if my faux pas had been a cue, Donald returned. 'Elisabeth, I should show you the house.'

I searched for Hilary's eyes, but she would not give them to me.

'Sorry,' I said.

My apology was spot on because Hilary nodded and managed the briefest of smiles.

Donald's pace was enthusiastic, and I had to hurry after him through the kitchen to a room which they probably called the breakfast room. Strangely, he didn't introduce me to the other guests, but they looked up as I passed, and we exchanged smiles. Donald came to a halt by the fireplace, its shoulder-height, purple marble mantlepiece dominating the room, a floor-standing Asian vase filled with pampas grass by its side. 'Hilary tells me you're very big in interior design.'

'Yes, and I know how important this house is.'

'Gosh, do you? I'm so pleased.'

I wasn't going to spoil it this time, I'd keep it upbeat. 'A Lutyens Arts and Crafts house is my absolute favourite.'

I prattled on about the house, keeping it firmly in the territory of professional interior designer meets owner of quasi-stately home who is wanting to be validated for buying a piece of English history. Then I mentioned the window seat and he immediately attuned.

'You must come and see it.' Donald turned immediately.

It seemed a little inappropriate to be leaving everyone, having not even said hello, to follow the male host upstairs. But Donald's enthusiasm gave me little choice.

167

The stairs were wide enough for both of us to walk side by side, the rise slight enough for it to feel graceful and relaxing. Away from the other guests, Donald's tempo slowed, and he put his arm around my waist. It felt paternal but at the same time a little intimate. He did know I was gay, didn't he? After all, they'd addressed the invitation to 'Elisabeth and Mary'. But maybe it was Hilary who'd sent it.

We reached the landing, walked the return to the end, and looked out over the garden. Donald was telling me about the garden, the history of its development, and the difficulties of finding gardeners, but I couldn't concentrate. Behind him I could see the window seat and as Donald spoke, I moved slowly towards it.

It was wide enough for a tall man to stretch out and probably deep enough to sleep on. Below the seat and on each side were masses of books, a small library. I pictured George leaning back against the plush cushions.

'Do you mind if I try it?'

Donald smiled. 'Please do, it's a lovely space, isn't it?'

I kicked off my shoes and sat, just as George had done, with my feet up. The seat was deeply padded, and I leant against the cushions. With only a small turn of the head one could look out of the window and still survey the hallway.

'You look very much at home,' Donald chuckled.

'I could spend all day here. And what a great idea having a library next to a reading space.'

'I'm so glad you like it. Look, have a moment here, while I go and freshen up your glass.'

Donald walked off, back in his quick-step. Now I was alone in George's world. I'd wanted to ask Donald about George, to know if these were his books, but I didn't want to make the same mistake as I had with Hilary.

My thoughts turned to the girl. When I was about fifteen, well into secondary school anyway, I stopped seeing George. This was a little before his accident. I started seeing a girl sitting on the window seat instead. Just like her brother before, constantly here, constantly reading.

It was this girl that made me realise, for sure, that I was gay. She was beautiful, with fine features and blonde hair. She was, how we would say back then, very trendy. New Romantic style, with dramatic make up and a different hairdo each month. She was tall but waif-like, and I'd realised that I wanted to kiss her, to be there on the window seat with her, fooling around. I was at that funny age, when I'd packed up my toys for good, cleared out the old children's books and was adding to my collection of romance and historical novels, week by week.

Before the appearance of the girl, my main fantasy was buying, or more importantly, living in Deauville du Coup. There would be a husband, children, a labrador and a very cheery cleaner who also cooked our meals. I never did have a cleaner or a dog. We have a very odd cat instead, who I'm sure considers Mary and I imposters.

At one time, there was a very slim possibility of a husband, but only because he was rich enough to buy the house of my dreams. He proposed in a torture of shyness, but I just giggled and tickled him, without having to formally turn him down. We are still friends.

Then I met my Mary, and that caused lots of disruption, as these things do, with my father being quite the dinosaur. But the disruption was worth it, and Mary and I are very happy together. We are that annoying couple that agree on everything and know each other's thoughts.

So, it was the young, blonde goddess in that very same

window that had crystalised my awareness of my sexuality. Where was she now? Why had Hilary avoided the question?

There were plenty of rumours about George's accident, that it wasn't a heart attack, as reported, but he'd been pushed down the stairs, or attacked by the dog and had fallen as he ran. But these explanations never rang true, and I dismissed them as the product of creative, undisciplined minds with too much time and not enough evidence. The principal source of these rumours was from the domestic staff who the Goldsmith's employed from the residents of Bemblebury, and there is the possibility that they filtered and spun a narrative that was not entirely flattering of their no doubt difficult employers.

What I did believe was that George had struggled with low self-esteem, and that Donald's parenting style had not suited the child's demeanour, that he'd been a challenging, aggressive father who wanted his son to hit the ground running, climb the career ladder and set the world on fire with bold choices, and with a similar energy and skill as his own business acumen. I'd say this would have been completely contrary to the boy's wishes or needs.

Other rumours were that he'd struggled to make friends and given up trying to go back to school. He'd failed in the sciences and mathematical subjects his father had pushed him towards, hated the sports and martial arts clubs his father had spent a small fortune on with private lessons. Apparently, from about the age of thirteen onwards, the Goldsmiths had holidayed on their own, without George. He was left behind with staff.

He did, however, have a foolproof method of escape from this difficult world. He was a reader and would disappear for hours with his books, not even greeting his mother or father upon their return home. It wasn't that he didn't like his parents, he just knew it was best to avoid the inevitable criticism and challenges that resulted from such a clash of personalities.

The variation to this rumour was that George was gay and that this wasn't welcomed by either his mother or father. Being the only son, he was expected to produce an heir. I'm not sure I believe that part. Surely the world has grown up? My dad didn't want me to be gay, but that had nothing to do with not being able to have grandchildren.

'George, tell me, how was it for you?' I said out loud. I plumped up a cushion and leaned back, pulled my feet up and hugged my knees. What was it really like for George? Not going to school only works if you have siblings or energetic parents taking you out to socialise. It must really suck if all you have is some demented dog, parents who don't like you and you live in the quiet part of a quiet village.

It was whilst pondering George that I first felt a presence. It was slight at first, just a feeling of someone else there, of not being alone anymore.

It was a warm feeling, not frightening, of being loved and held, of being admired, and hugged.

I'd had a gin, but this was different. At first, I thought it was the elation of finally achieving my goal and entering the house, but the feeling grew to something euphoric, like coming home to a loving family at Christmas. Of being received with open arms, a big smile and earnest interest in my wellbeing. It was like being greeted by my cat, who has been waiting all day for me to come home and is looking forward to spending time together.

I don't usually have those kinds of intuitive feelings. Mary does, frequently. She calls herself an empath.

Nothing to do with reiki or crystals, she'd call that woo, but she does believe that she reads people well, picking up on their micro-behaviours and reading between their words.

Once or twice we've fallen out when she insists that I'm not telling her everything, that I'm not being entirely truthful, but I'm not keeping anything from her. It's just that she knows me better that I know myself and when I'm not answering that universal question, 'How are you?' accurately, she's on to me.

Then I realised who this presence was—George. I wasn't frightened, I was excited.

'Gosh, you do look very serene.' Donald was back, thrusting another gin into my hands. Sitting down on the window seat by my feet, he bizarrely put a hand on my ankle, just briefly, but even so. 'Hilary was saying you grew up here. We didn't realise.'

It took a moment to break away from George. 'Yes, I moved away for university, then I was in London, where I met Mary, and we followed our careers.' I felt the need to emphasise my connection with another woman. 'But last year I persuaded Mary we should move to the country and when I showed her around Bemblebury, she was sold.'

'Or old Roger's house was sold.' Donald snorted. 'It's a lovely old property,' he said more seriously. 'You've done well.'

Donald began a soliloquy about planning permission, about how difficult it was to get a good cleaner, and I gradually switched off as the feeling of George returned. He wasn't so happy now. I sensed a latent anxiety, some hostility to his father, I supposed.

My heart was beating faster, as if it were beating for both George and me. The feeling was so strong I lost track of what Donald was saying.

'Would you?' he asked.

Oops, I'd completely missed Donald's question.

'Sorry?'

'Would you like a tour of the rest of the upstairs.'

'That would be lovely, yes please, and I suppose there are attic rooms too?'

'No, that's just for storage.'

I was too excited to argue, but that didn't ring true.

I was not disappointed. Each bedroom had hand-printed silk damask wallpaper, floor-length drapery, original fireplaces, exquisite tiling, leaded windows, tall, ogee skirting, and even the electrical fittings were thirties style. The master bedroom had a solid wood, double sleigh bed, pale oak writing desk and a sumptuous sofa.

I glanced through the door of the fourth bedroom and noticed that it was both half the size of the others and looked more like a boxroom. I was about to move on when I sensed that feeling again, this time much stronger than before. I stepped into the room and was immediately aware of a happy feeling of companionship, the pleasure of being with someone likeminded. I was truly lost in the tranquil moment. I hadn't known quite by how much until Donald offered, 'Gosh, I can tell you're really very happy here. Look why not stay a while, take a seat and enjoy the ambience.'

I heard the doorbell.

'Please excuse me, I'd better get that,' Donald said. Again, there was the excuse to touch me, and he squeezed the back of my arm.

I sat on the bed and looked around. This must have been George's room. There were no toys, no childish wallpaper or playful carpet. Very few clues to say it was ever a young teenager's bedroom. No, I just felt it. Where was all this coming from? I don't have these kinds of feelings. It wasn't a male presence, or at least, not a macho one. This was a gentle soul, convivial, light-hearted. I thought of singing, of dancing, of playing a game of hide and seek. I thought of my own childhood and the fun I'd had, of the times where I'd met someone new and hit it off. I'd found a friend.

Time must have passed, and I'd completely lost track of it. I bathed in that warm and fuzzy feeling, somewhat surprised that George would be so gentle, that our connection could feel so engaging.

'Elisabeth?'

Mary was in front of me, holding a glass of wine and looking worried. 'Are you okay? What are you doing up here?'

I stood up and gave her a kiss.

'I told you this morning, I've always wanted to see this house.' I sat back down.

'Yeah, yeah, I know but you seem fazed and there's a whole load of more interesting rooms, especially the ones with people in them.'

'It's wonderful, everything I'd hoped it would be.'

Then I felt a new feeling. I felt it in my stomach, as if the floor had moved away. There was anger, distrust. Not mine, but from the presence of George. It felt like I was in the middle of the playground, trying to persuade him that everything was okay.

'He doesn't want you here,' I said.

'Sorry!'

'Mary, do you feel it?'

She looked at me mystified and worried. I waited.

Then she nodded, 'Yeah, kind of,' she whispered.

'It's George.'

'Yeah, you told me about him.'

I watched as she processed the situation, her face now more worried and watching me open-mouthed. She took a couple of steps toward me but stopped abruptly.

The feeling now was more like a pain around my heart, a tension, a squeezing. That must have played out on my face.

Mary looked sad and disappointed, but I felt I couldn't placate her. I couldn't placate either of them.

She took a step back. 'Is it better if I go downstairs?'

I nodded.

'Join me when you can.' Mary turned on her heel and left the room. It was just me and George now. The tension lifted and I felt the heavy emotions lighten. I hadn't realised, but I must have been holding my breath. I exhaled deeply and then took a deep breath in. My skin seemed electrified, as though I could sense everything in the room, the furniture, the bed, even the shadow behind the door. George had spent a lot of time here. Something of him had remained.

I stayed like that for nearly half an hour, and it was exhausting. I heard nothing, said nothing, but I continued to reassure him: everything is okay. Mary has gone, it's just you and me.

Finally, I spoke out loud to the room. 'I should really go downstairs; they'll wonder where I've gone.'

George was not happy. I sensed the energy changing into a powerful feeling of disappointment, that the original happy moment we'd shared was gone.

Slowly, I began to feel I could leave the room and stepped out into the hallway. When I passed the window seat, I stood awhile. Outside it was dark, but thanks to the street lighting I could make out the gate.

'I'll try and come back,' I said out loud, and slowly. I was released and left the quiet intimacy of that space. I walked down the wide and formal staircase into the adulthood playground of gossip, drinking and carefully chosen words, exchanges with more serious consequences.

I only had half an hour to meet some of the guests before the party wound up. Mary and I gave our thanks to the hosts and walked into the cold evening air. As we reached the gate, I looked back at the window seat, almost expecting to see George. It was, of course, empty.

We had a giggle walking through the woods. Mary had driven straight to the party from work, had had a drink and didn't want to drive. We spoke loudly to each other as if preventing the onset of anxiety from the eerie darkness. George wasn't a topic of conversation until we were home. It was an unspoken pact, to not speak of presences, let alone a ghost, in the half-moon of a cloudy night, in a quiet wood with just an owl screeching. It could have turned a spooky moment into something quite frightening. But with the front door closed, Mary lost no time.

She took my coat. 'What was all that about, upstairs?'

I explained my feelings from when they'd first materialised, the sense of joy on the window seat to the changing mood when first Donald and then Mary had arrived. She listened silently, not passing any comment or judgement.

My phone rang.

'Elisabeth? It's Donald. I have a proposal for you. I was going to explain at the party, but I wanted you to see the house first and make sure you liked it.'

Donald moved as swiftly in conversation as he had walked through the house. He explained that they were thinking of selling and wanted me to write a house history, the usual kind of article I'd write for a magazine. When they'd bought Deauville du Coup all those years ago, he was sold just by reading the estate agent's particulars. But not only had the Goldsmiths lost them, but because they'd done so much work, they needed something up to date and of the moment.

I was thrilled and accepted immediately. I couldn't conceal my enthusiasm, and although it's a lot more professional to retain one's equanimity, this was a wonderful opportunity. We arranged for me to visit them in the morning. My very next thought was that it would be a chance to connect with George again. The evening could not have gone better.

Mary, however, was a little quiet for the rest of it. She thought I'd missed out by not talking with the other guests. Was she jealous, I wondered. Maybe I didn't quite explain my experience properly. I knew it was unusual, and I hadn't described it as weird, it was a special intimacy. I didn't say that phrase to Mary, she wouldn't have understood, or have liked to have heard it.

We were both tired and were soon in bed.

Chapter Two

Mary was distant in the morning.

We lay in bed drinking our tea in silence. I tried a couple of times to get her chatting, and finally I hit the right trigger. 'I'd thought I'd blown it last night. First I dug a hole for myself with Hilary and then I must have come across as really weird to Donald, when I was preoccupied with George's presence, whatever that was.'

Mary sighed, gulped back her coffee and got out of bed. 'I think you'll find that's why we were invited, so you can help sell their house for a super-inflated price. He'll have your article published in House and Garden magazine and splashed across the Sunday Times property section. They'll probably get Kevin McCloud to do some retrospective presentation.'

I decided to get to Deauville du Coup and leave Mary to work out her mood.

When I arrived, my experience of the equanimity of humanity did not improve. As I stepped up to the front door, I could hear the Goldsmiths going at each other, Hilary dismissive and disparaging, Donald patronising and sweetly condescending. I quickly rang the bell, hoping to keep my inner peace intact.

Hilary gave the briefest of hellos. I think she realised I'd overheard them. There was no evidence of last night's party. Perhaps the wreckage had been hidden away in the kitchen. Donald suggested that I work in his study, but I requested the window seat, and he didn't argue.

'Of course, go and make yourself comfortable. I'll bring coffee.'

The window seat was like a magnet for me. I expected

to feel George as soon as I sat down and was disappointed when I didn't. As I waited for Donald I began to wonder if last night's event had been entirely in my head.

I studied the books more closely, which was a lot easier with the morning sun streaming through. They really were very dull titles. Where were George's books? These can't have been his, they were all over a hundred years old, chosen purely for their leather and gilt bindings. Titles that promised much but failed to deliver when you opened them, filled with anachronistic references and people you've never heard of. They belonged in a museum.

Where were the books he relished, that kept him on the window seat? There were many hobbies he could have taken up that were quiet and insular, but he'd chosen reading. I always wondered what he was reading and surely now I would be able to find out, but not from these shelves.

It was George who inspired me to read. When I saw him, hour after hour, with his face stuck in a book, it didn't seem peculiar to me that I should do the same. When my father complained that I had my head in a book again, I knew that was just Dad and there was nothing wrong with me.

Donald suddenly sat down next to me. There's something about the way he moved that was quiet and secretive, like a snake.

'You're looking very fresh this morning, like an English rose.'

He was going to put his hand on my knee, but I quickly straightened myself up. Men don't know how to respond to a woman completely disinterested in them. They either attempt the impossible or treat you like a bloke. Is it because they're frightened by something that they can't control?

Donald had brought me a cup of coffee, but then he sprang up and went into the bedroom. Within seconds he was out again with a fold-out card table.

'This'll make your endeavours more effective.' He put the table in front of me. 'Ah, yes, and the box of goodies. Give me a minute.'

Donald slithered away while I put my laptop on the table and set up my writing space. Hopefully in this "box of goodies" were the ingredients I needed to create a juicy article. A house history without facts is just an endless list of superlatives and cliché-swamped diarrhoea; readers wouldn't make it past the first paragraph. My secret was drawing on the past masters of architectural description. I have the complete forty-six volumes of *Pevsner's Houses of England and Wales*, signed first editions. It takes up two shelves and is separately listed on our house contents insurance.

Donald plonked a portable A4 document safe on the table.

'This is a treasure chest; you'll get yourself all hot and bothered with this stuff.'

Donald clearly didn't have a clue what would get me hot and bothered, only, it seemed, what would get me hot and irritated.

I didn't look up. 'Wonderful, leave it with me.'

I waited until he'd gone before opening the box. I wasn't disappointed. They still had the original letters between client and architect. Not the letters to Lutyens but the handwritten drafts. There were blueprints, builders' quotes, land analysis. This was indeed a treasure and would elevate my article to something that might even make the national press.

Deauville de Coup was an important house and I really wanted to demonstrate that for my own ends. Although the Goldsmiths would benefit financially, I wanted to display not only my own professional excellence, but how this house was one of England's overlooked gems.

Within half an hour, documents covered the table, the whole of the window seat and many square metres of the floor in front of me, yet my notes page was blank. There were just too many important facts to list...where to start?

But then my investigation took a curious distraction. I found a whole letter, a drawing, and a detailed specification, all stapled together, just for the window seat. This was the ultimate delicacy and I consumed it with delight.

The letter, written by the husband of the client, requested a library and reading space overlooking the garden, large enough to hold his wife's collection of antique books.

Then, the sentence that put the creation of my article on hold: the shelves must contain a secret cupboard for the most prized book of the collection, the journal of Louis XVI.

I had to find this hidden cupboard.

The drawing was a diagram, showing the construction and hidden mechanism, hiding both the opening and hinge of what would be a very heavy shelf. However, it didn't illuminate where, in all the shelving, the cupboard was located.

The idea of hidden and secret spaces delights me, and fortunately there are many examples to be found amongst the inventory of Britain's stately homes. Yet my favourite has to be in the Doge's Palace in Venice. Mary and I were there for the weekend and had booked an exclusive tour, enticingly described as a chance to explore the parts of the palace the majority of tourists never see. It included a room Napoleon had personally requested to be built which contained not one but two secret doors. The room is only three by two metres, yet despite being in there listening to the guide for five minutes, we'd not spotted the two doors. The first hid a stairwell that led to a tiny prison cell, and the other, on the opposite side of the room, a door to the Doge's residence via his personal, private terrace. The doors were hidden in the panelling. They were normal sized doors, no small feat to disguise. When the doors were opened, we both gasped as the passageways were revealed.

I began a detailed search of the window seat's library, looking for the tell-tale signs: a butt hinge, a worn piece of veneer, a keyhole or a moulding that is cut short. I took off my shoes and stood on the window seat; maybe the cupboard was up high to make entry even more difficult.

'Is this going in the article?' Hilary said, startling me as she appeared behind me.

'Yes, it's really interesting…' I stopped myself. Hilary didn't need to know about the cupboard, not until I'd found it. Unless, of course, she already knew. 'Part of the specification of the house was this window seat and compact library for an important collection.'

'Hmm, that is interesting.'

Hilary seemed genuine.

'Well, these books did come with the house, but then, of course, we aren't the first owners.'

'Have you found any special books?' I asked.

'I'm afraid we haven't looked; other projects have got in the way. They are a beautiful and original feature so they can stay.' Hilary chuckled. 'Sorry, that does sound shallow. Donald and I are readers, but these books look…quite uninteresting.'

This was all I needed to know. If she was going to tell me about a secret cupboard, she would have done it by now.

I was then drawn into a long conversation of Hilary's trials and tribulations with interior design. I listened politely but itched to get back to my search. Then, just as she was trailing off, Donald appeared, and he added his favourite anecdotes to the saga of their role as guardians of Deauville du Coup. Hilary did, however, do some of my work for me and asked Donald if he'd found any special books. But this too drew a blank.

After forty minutes I was released and promised a top up of my coffee. As soon as they were gone, I hunted low and high, standing back to look for irregularities in the proportions and lengths of shelves. But to no avail; the carpenter had done his work well.

When Donald came back with my coffee he invited me to see the picture gallery at the rear of the second floor. I hadn't seen this the previous night, having been preoccupied with George in his old bedroom. The picture gallery was amazing, containing a wonderful collection of limited prints and original oils. I didn't recognise the artist, but they were exquisite. Donald and Hilary both had a good eye for art.

On the way back I spotted the disguised door to the attic rooms. I've seen enough of these in stately homes to know what to look for, and they're quite easy to spot as the depth of the walls doesn't make sense. I planned to return but didn't say anything to Donald. His dismissive explanation that the attic was just a dusty old storage area was ridiculous. The wonderfully celebrated dormer windows next to the fabulously tall chimneys and set within an impossibly steep roof could only mean one thing: at least one room was up there, if not a whole suite of accommodation.

Donald suggested I have lunch with them in the garden, but I quickly side-stepped and explained I'd work through so I could get back to Mary and have some time with her before the end of the day.

This, apparently, was his opportunity to pass comment on our relationship.

'You make a very fair couple. Congratulations on finding each other.'

What is it about being gay that makes people feel their approval or disapproval should be voiced?

One comment we often get, amongst our gay friends, is that we are a 'couple of queens'. We take it in good humour, it's funny. But Mary Queen of Scots and Elizabeth I, did not have a good relationship whilst my Mary and I definitely do.

Before disappearing again, Donald told me the price he was hoping to achieve for the house. It was five times higher than what Mary and I had just spent buying our little three-bedroom house in the posh part of Bemblebury. Donald explained that they were hoping to start their retirement back in London, because although he worked in the city, he'd never found time to enjoy it.

Finally, Donald walked off downstairs, and I could return to my hunt. I spent another half an hour meticulously tracing each edge of all the shelves, bringing books away from the sides to see if they hid something. Perhaps it had been planned but never built. I plumped up a cushion and leaned back, taking in the garden lit by the glory of full sunshine.

My mind wandered, reminiscing about my school days,

the endless back and forth to and from school. This must have triggered George as, suddenly, he was back inside my head.

He was giggling, something had tickled his funny bone. Maybe because, like me, he'd been wondering if last night had really happened. His presence wasn't so much of a shock this time and I allowed him to enter my consciousness fully.

He didn't waste any time. My mind's imagination was now being shared, mixing with his. I was absorbing George's vision, his memory, and I saw an image with great clarity. A book, a bookshelf, the window seat; we were standing back facing it. Then towards the left, down by our feet on the bottom shelf, we lifted the top of the shelf just above the books and the whole shelf swivelled out like a door.

Now my mind was all my own again. He'd gone, but I sensed he was not far away and was watching me.

I listened for sounds of Hilary or Donald and peered down the stairs for them. Guessing the coast was clear, I bent down and looked at the shelf George had shown me. Putting my hand under the top of the shelf and pulling, nothing happened. Momentarily I was disappointed, but then I tried again, this time lifting the shelf as well. I heard a click, then pulled again and the shelf slid towards me. I pulled it right out. Inside, a small cavity was revealed, as long as the bookshelf but not very deep. A single book lay there and I grabbed it.

Having double checked there was nothing else inside the cupboard, I quickly closed it. My heart was pounding, the excitement enough to make me hold my breath. What was this book? It certainly wasn't Louis XVI's journal.

Taking up my usual position facing the top of the

staircase, just in case Donald sneaked up on me, I pulled up my laptop and used its screen to shield my find. The pages were filled with handwriting, drawings and glued-in magazine clippings. Amazing! No, this wasn't Louis' journal, this was George's.

This was everything I could have dreamed of. I would understand George better than anyone, probably even his parents. Then came the paralysis of inner conflict: shouldn't I be making a proper start on writing my article? And was it morally wrong to withhold the discovery of my find from the Goldsmiths? Whether it was right to read the private journal was not an issue at all, as George had shown me where his journal was; he wanted me to read it. This final thought cured my indecision and for the next hour I was engrossed in reading his diary.

I read it feverishly. No deadline had been given to me by Donald, and for that matter neither had we discussed money. Either way, I was supposed to be working, and at any minute access to the journal might prove difficult.

George's writing style was compulsive. He was articulate and intimate. The diary was his confidante and disclosed everything. There was a self-awareness and maturity beyond his years.

"I'm sure it's not supposed to be like this. I have no one to talk things through with, not the cook or the cleaner. You can tell they just want to gossip."

Then a gut-wrenching revelation: "Mum and Dad talk to each other as if the other is the most loathed person in the universe. Dad swears at her as loud as he can, with words I've only read in books. Mum doesn't shout but quietly and accurately points out Dad's inabilities, and sniggers as if he's worthless."

But then something I'd not heard in the rumours: "The

family don't visit anymore. They don't write either. I could write to Aunt Helen, but she's probably forgotten me by now."

A sadness: "I should have stayed at school of course. I should have been braver. School is supposed to be difficult, I just gave up too easily. I could have had loads of friends. But now I'll never know."

I turned page after page, confessions, hopes, fears: "I know I'm different. You can't blame people for not liking me. People are afraid of what they don't understand. I should try and be more like them. But of course, I never can. I'll always be the one they point at."

He wanted to be Davina McCall, "because she's so funny, confident, and is determined to be everything and have everything she wants in life. She is everything I am not."

Then my heart fluttered. It was just a paragraph but even so, the words gave my schooldays a twist. "The girl is different now, the one that passes every day; she's at secondary school. There's a sassiness about her, with her Cindy Lauper hair and her Madonna lace, fingerless gloves. She's always been gorgeous but now she's turning into a woman. Naturally, with no effort. That's the nature of real beauty, it's effortless. She'll have boyfriends soon, if not already. She looks up at me, sitting in the window. God! Does she fancy me? If only she knew! I should go down there and introduce myself and ask her to play. God no, ha ha—ask her to just come and talk. We're adults now. I remember her from school. She was one of the rare, nice ones".

I was elated and at the same time joyous, but above all I felt a certain amount of relief that my childhood infatuation with this boy and house was not so one-sided.

It made sense, of course. So many things in the real world are like that. It's never like you're in a bubble, you're always subject to a wider dynamic. If you think something is just happening to you then you're just in your head. George and I were part of each other's lives, he'd been as fascinated with me as much as I'd been fascinated by him.

Then I turned a page and saw the sweetest thing. He'd glued a photograph of his sister, the beautiful girl I'd seen later on, onto the page. They must have really gelled for him to celebrate her like that; friends, not just brother and sister. It was a fabulous photograph, like a studio portrait, with full make up. This was the vision of a goddess that had made me realise it was girls I fancied, not boys.

What kind of relationship did they have? I hoped so much that she'd brought solace and friendship to his troubled soul. I guess she must have gone to the grammar school and been driven there by her parents because I never saw her at secondary school or on the bus.

Hearing the soft pad of footsteps, I sensed it was Donald slinking up. I put the journal under my laptop and prepared for his invasion.

'How's it all going?'

'Very good. Yes, I'm making good progress.'

'Good, good.'

Donald was still standing there waiting for details.

'I've been considering the right flavour for the article.' I said, attempting professionalism from a mind which, at that moment, was anything but. 'I want to capture the reader's attention right from the start with a title that's intriguing. Maybe Deauville du Coup: the Art of a Genius, the Craft of a Gentleman.'

'Gosh, yes, I like that very much.'

I looked at my phone; it was four. 'I didn't realise it was

so late.'

'Well, don't rush off on our part. It's Saturday night but we're just having a quiet night in.'

'No, I promised Mary I'd get back early. Shall I come tomorrow?'

'Yes, great, I'd love to get the thing done. I realise we haven't spoken about money.'

'If it's good enough to get into Homes and Gardens, with a slightly different bent for the Sunday Times, maybe you'll consider a bonus.'

'Absolutely. If you can achieve that we'd be over the moon. Think of a figure and email it to me.'

I wrapped things up with Donald and made my excuses to have the space to myself for a little longer before I left. I wanted to put the journal back in its treasure chest. When Donald had gone, I quickly stowed it away, tucking in one of the documents I'd found earlier as a bookmark.

As I shut the shelf, George's presence returned to me. He seemed anxious; was it because I was leaving? I leaned back against the cushion and spent a moment reconnecting, thinking of his passage in the journal, his homage to me, and remembering, appreciating, how special that was. In my head I voiced, 'Don't worry, I'll be back tomorrow.' I was immediately rewarded with the sense that George was now in a light and happy mood.

As I looked from Lutyens' masterfully crafted window, I imagined what George had seen: a young girl in school uniform walking past, with the sassiness of Lauper and Madonna.

I giggled.

*

Mary and I spent our own quiet evening together. We hadn't completed our unpacking, and recently we'd made a new routine of doing this together and choosing where things should go. In the past I might have done this on my own but doing it together has brought us even closer. She defers to my interior design skills, but at the same time I will want to celebrate her choice and we'll have a mini battle of wills deferring to each other, trying to demonstrate our love for each other. We end up tickling and hugging and, of course, eventually in bed. I love her very much.

*

The next morning Mary was in a better mood and had a relaxing and social day planned. I wasn't going to speak of George, because I felt that it might make her jealous. But she knows how much he and the house mean to me and when I left for Deauville de Coup, she bid me, "have fun with each other". I almost jogged through the woods, I was so eager to get back to reading his diary.

The Goldsmiths' Sunday routine was clearly a lie in as Hilary answered the door in her bathrobe. It was almost 11.30. She promised to bring coffee and without waiting to be invited, I proceeded upstairs. The card table and box of documents were still there by the window seat, and I reassembled my makeshift office. As soon as I heard Hilary running her bath, I retrieved the diary. I leaned back against the cushion and took a moment to connect with George and his youthful spirit.

Connecting with him brought back memories of my home life when I was young. Back then, I enjoyed time with friends and family, but I also cherished the moments on my own, lost in my thoughts as I walked to school. It was my daily meditation. I was lucky to have had this contrast. I had a choice, but George only had his insular world.

I opened the journal and realised immediately that my bookmark had changed position. Who'd been here? I looked up, alarmed. Was Donald spying on me? The bookmark was now almost at the end of the journal.

"Dad's put me in the attic so I can't be seen at the window anymore. But I like the space, it's quirky. Dad has spent money on new carpets, and I've decorated it, but I miss my view over the garden and watching people pass by. Will I ever see the girl in the school uniform again?"

Then I heard George read with me, quietly at first, but gradually his voice took over. How quietly he spoke, how sad he sounded.

"I don't bother coming down in the day, maybe only for a sandwich, and not until Dad is back from work. Mum is wrapped up anyway with climbing her little ladder up the community hierarchy, the bridge club, arranging the village fete, being the lady of the manor. We don't really talk anymore."

I felt a tightness in my chest. George was moving from sad to hopeless, to frustration and nearing anger. Why him? What went wrong? Why hadn't school worked out for him? Why was he different?

I leant back and thought of George in the window and the time when I stopped seeing him every day. Was that when he went to the attic?

Where was his sister in all this? Perhaps she was more of a social animal and didn't have time for George. I read on, looking for clues, but instead George took over. My mind was being filled with what he saw: his memories. *He is walking up the stairs, walking past the window seat to the secret attic door, he lifts, it opens. It has the same mechanism as the bookshelf. He climbs the stairs to the attic. He wants me to follow.*

I put the journal away as I knew what I had to do. But this wasn't the right time, I'd have to wait for the moment I wouldn't be missed. Right on cue, I heard Donald climb the stairs. I spread open the box and pulled out a few documents, trying to look busy.

'Good morning, making an early start?' Donald chuckled. 'Earlier than us, anyway.'

He passed me my coffee.

'We'll be heading off shortly, but you stay and do your thing.'

Good, this was my chance. But first, I actually started writing my article. I filled the floor space with documents again, creating an ambience of a busy writer earnest in the endeavour of capturing the perfect house history. Within twenty minutes I'd filled two sides with notes, a rough outline.

The Goldsmiths called out from the front door, 'Help yourself to coffee, we'll see you later.' And I watched them as they walked down their drive.

Swiftly I moved to the attic door and, as George had shown me, lifted it, putting my fingers under the beading, I heard the click and the weight of the door made it open. It swung out towards me.

My heart was racing once more, and I climbed the steps. The attic room before me was an open plan affair, with not even a balustrade between the bedroom and the stairwell. George had made it his own, with posters, letters, and memorabilia stuck onto the wall. They seemed to have left George's room as it was when he died and not tidied him away.

And then I found his bookshelf, displaying the titles I'd hoped for: A definition in counterculture: biographies of prominent revolutionaries of thought; Orwell's *1984;* Kerouac's, *On the Road; Fear and Loathing in Las Vegas* by Hunter S. Thompson. This was completely different to my bookshelf, which had been packed with Dickens and Hardy, D H Lawrence and Edgar Allen Poe. Imagine the conversations we would have had. I saw the difference as a positive, and imagined George and I trading ideas, showing each other our different worlds.

But then, on the shelf next to his bed, there seemed a whole different kind of genre: Jan Morris' *Conundrum;* Virginia Wolf's *Orlando; Myra Breckinridge*, it's dust cover explaining that it was a satirical novel written by Gore Vidal; *Man into Woman* by Lili Elbe. What were these titles all about?

I stepped around to a dressing table beneath the window, which I saw, with surprise, was covered in similar paraphernalia to my own: hairbrushes, make up, hair bands. Was this George's room or his sister's?

It was beginning to sink in, but not until I saw a photograph on the wall was I sure. The A4 size photo was of George, but magazine clippings of a dress, earrings and blonde hair were stuck on his image. In large letters at the bottom of the photo, cut out letters spelled out a name: Georgina.

George had been the beautiful woman I'd seen in the window. There was no sister.

Chapter Three

It felt like panic, but it was just confusion; decades of perceptions of George were cascading and jumbling, forming a new understanding of who he was.

Now that I had this new possibility, that he wanted to be a girl, a woman, many more questions arose. Was that why there was a rumour in the village he was gay? Is that why Hilary had looked so traumatised when I'd asked about her daughter? I needed answers, and they were probably in the diary.

I went back down to the window seat, retrieved the journal and opened it back to where the bookmark had moved to. And that was another question: who had moved the bookmark last night?

Georgina was back in my head, stronger now. Moving my fingers to turn the pages, we moved on three days, stopping at an entry with the heading: Why is the World So Angry with Me? "I'm still recovering from Dad's shouting, 'What do you think you're doing? The whole village could have seen you in that wig and dress. People aren't accepting of this behaviour, it's probably illegal.' It was alright for me, apparently, because I never went out, but they had to show their faces in the village."

As my fingers turned the pages, Georgina read to me, impersonating Donald: "Another rant from Dad, 'Mother told me what you've been up to, wearing makeup, her dresses, her underwear!' He was shaking his fist at me. He was mad, red faced with it. 'You'll stay in your room when I go to work, you'll not come down till I'm back.'"

I could feel my chest tightening, as if Donald was squeezing my heart. "'That's the last time! Before I leave each day, I want you in your room. Take what you need for the day because I'll be locking you up there.' Dad wasn't listening. I pleaded, I tried to explain, but he just turned his back on me."

I closed the journal and put it away. How much time did I have before the Goldsmiths returned? I walked quickly back up to Georgina's attic bedroom and searched for more clues. What really happened back then?

The window looked out over the village. You could see as far as the cricket field and the pub car park, and then the rooftop of the school. It must have been torture for Georgina to see this and not be able to be part of it, to not want to go out and be seen as a man, when she felt like a woman. The daily frustration, the loneliness, the anger of her parents refusing to accept her as she was, must have been unbearable.

My breath became short, my vision was blurring. I needed air, and I had to get out of the attic bedroom. Slowly, I walked back down the narrow stairwell, feeling unsteady. When I got to the door and pushed, it wouldn't open. Georgina's memories filled my head, a memory of her pushing the door and not being able to get out. I sat down. She'd pushed and pushed, screaming 'Dad, Dad, Dad, please let me out.'

I must have fainted.

When I came round, the door was open, and Donald was standing in front of me.

'I thought I'd made myself clear, Elisabeth. The attic rooms are only for storage, so you don't need to be here.'

I looked at him, unable to hide my thoughts, and he must have realised: I knew he'd locked his son in the attic. That was most probably when the accident had happened. George had had some kind of heart attack, and no one was

195

there to call an ambulance.

Donald opened the door wide and took a step back. 'Please, get your things. The deal's off.'

*

Within the hour, I was back home trying to make sense of it.

Mary supplied cups of tea and nursed me as I sat on the sofa by the fire.

What just happened?

Eventually Mary gave up waiting and tried to tease out of me why I was back early and why I was so tense. I'd lost the power of articulation; even the usual translation and interpretation skills of one's spouse were not enough for Mary to understand me this time. I must have sounded like an idiot.

Mary tried to summarise. 'So, the girl you fancied was the boy you'd always seen reading in the window. But the boy wanted to be a girl, and this freaked out the father and he locked him up to hide his shame. George freaked out from being locked up and had an anxiety attack and that brought on a heart attack which killed him. Which everyone now is calling an accident.'

'Thank you, yes, I think that's what happened.'

Mary put another log on the fire and made me another tea. We sat in silence, letting the ramifications of it all sink in. 'So,' Mary started, 'she, they-

'Let's call her Georgina.'

'Georgina fancied you?'

'Yes, there is that.'

'What are you going to do? Do you think Hilary knows what really happened?'

'I don't know, I can't really go back and ask.'

'How did you leave it with them then?

'I got sacked. My input is no longer required.'

'Is that fair? You were working on it for a day and a half.'

I laughed, 'No, I was conducting my own research. I don't think you can call what I did work.'

'Just go back then and see what Hilary knows.'

'I can't. Donald made it quite clear he doesn't want me there. I even tried flirting with him, to bring him round.'

'You did what?' Mary giggled.

'I know he fancies me, so I put my hand on his arm and said how well I thought we'd been getting on and it would be nice to get to know him better.'

We both laughed and this broke the tension.

'Go back tomorrow,' Mary said. 'Donald will be at work, and you can make sure Hilary realises that he brought this all about. Who in this day and age locks up their children?'

*

I'd left it until after lunch, but Hilary was still in her bathrobe, looking like she had no intention of getting dressed for the day.

Her greeting was uncomfortable, or more accurately, she didn't greet me. She couldn't even look me in the eyes. It had been Donald that had dismissed me, she'd lurked downstairs, probably too embarrassed.

On the way to Deauville du Coup, I'd made a plan: she was either going to tell me to leave or she'd be interested, her response wasn't in my control.

Hilary showed me in and before closing the door looked

down the drive, as if checking if any of her neighbours had seen her accept me in.

The awkwardness grew. Hilary wasn't bothering with any pleasantries but led me to the kitchen. I couldn't read her; was she angry or inquisitive? Her hair, for once, was a complete mess. Even if she wasn't going to get dressed, surely she could have run a brush through her hair? Then I noticed her wrist. It looked like she'd been rubbing it severely. Did Hilary have some kind of anxiety condition herself?

She stopped at the bar stool where we'd stood two nights before, looking almost as if she were going to finish our conversation.

'You know, then, that I don't have a daughter,' she said quietly. Finally, she connected with my eyes. 'Tea or coffee? Or maybe something a little stronger?'

I didn't want to be rude, and maybe a drink is what Hilary needed to tackle what must have been a very difficult subject. 'I'll have whatever you're having.'

Hilary walked stiffly to the cupboard, her slippers padding on the tiled floor. I wondered if she was battling a hangover.

How should I start this difficult conversation? Was it wrong to wrench her out of the comfort of her ignorance by telling her that her son's death had not been an accident?

Before I could resolve this question, I heard a bottle being uncorked. Although she had her back to me, I saw her lift down a bottle of Courvoisier and pour. She turned and walked back with two large glasses.

Hilary passed me my glass and held hers up towards me. 'I feel you are about to make some major revelation. Have you come to save my soul?'

Again, I couldn't read her. Was this sarcasm or hostility?

'I just thought you should know what I found yesterday.'

'In your exploration of the attic?'

'Did you realise how angry Donald was with George?'

'You deduced this from the attic?'

'From Goerge's diary.'

For the first time, Hilary showed some inquisitiveness. 'George didn't leave a diary.'

'It wasn't in the attic, it was in the bookcase,' I watched Hilary process this information; she seemed unsure of herself now, 'and it spoke of Donald's anger.'

'Yes.' Hilary said, flatly.

'For what exactly? Because George was in the window dressed as a woman?'

Hilary smiled and felt for the stool behind her. In silence, she stepped up onto it without looking around. She sat on the stool and looked at the glass of brandy. 'Why would he be angry?'

Was this a rhetorical question? 'I suppose he was ashamed.'

Hilary smiled again. 'Gosh, I didn't realise Donald had a temper, and after all, why should he be ashamed? It's not as though he had to face the bridge club, or the W.I.'

I was confused. Was this a ruse to distract or an explanation?

She continued, 'But thank you for bringing it to my attention. Let's drink to that, shall we? Down in one?'

Hilary swigged back her brandy, and I followed, welcoming not only some relief from the tension, but feeling obliged to comply.

'Elisabeth, I'd like to show you something in the attic.

Would you come with me?'

'Yes of course.' This was a good sign; I'd gained her trust.

'But listen, no one knows about this and I don't want any pictures, so would you mind leaving your phone behind?'

'Yes of course.' I immediately took out my phone and put it on the counter.

I followed Hilary out of the kitchen, under the dozen or so servant bells above the door, into the breakfast room with the curtains majestically framing the impossibly tall windows. The sofa cushions, immaculately lined up in alternate colours, appeared to be forbidding anyone to sit down.

Hilary was going even faster than Donald had, and we were soon in the hallway with its handsome handprinted wallpaper. I registered the highly polished banister, the original and undamaged stair rods. Above the window seat, the glass in the windows appeared crystal clear, and through them I saw the manicured lawn and the hedges regimented like an architect's drawing.

We climbed the stairs to George's bedroom. I didn't need to show Hilary how to open its secret door. We stood in front of his bed, and I realised how out of breath I was. I felt faint and my heart was beating rapidly.

In that moment I looked around George's room. It was a riot, with its gaudy bedspread, wonky, unframed posters, and his library indicating a prelude to a public protest.

'This house.' I said, 'It's perfect, isn't it? Everything in your life is just so.'

'Yes, and George just didn't fit in.'

'And Georgina was beautiful, and maybe that was difficult for you too.'

The room was spinning, yet I felt a certain clarity. 'He didn't lock the door to keep George in, did he?'

'No, I rather think he wanted to keep me out.' She chuckled quietly, 'He'd do anything to keep George safe.'

And with that, Hilary turned to face me, putting a finger against my solar plexus. 'Dear Elisabeth, you should be careful what you drink. I don't think you can take it.'

She pushed gently and I collapsed onto the bed. Everything was too much now, and I just wanted to sleep.

Georgina was in my head again. 'Careful of Mum,' she was saying, and as I tried to work out why my legs felt strange, she said 'Please burn my diary.'

I had to get to her diary, but getting up was so difficult. I put my feet on the ground, but I couldn't work out how to get up.

'I don't want to get anyone into trouble,' Georgina continued.

I couldn't work out where Hilary had gone to.

Walking was impossible, so I got down on all fours and crawled to the stairs. Everything was blurry.

'I do love my parents. I know you don't think so, but they were all I ever had.'

Sitting on my bottom, I went down the steps to the door one step at a time. There'd been a lot of brandy in the glass, but it didn't explain my incapacity.

Finally, I got to the door; I needed that diary. But the door wouldn't budge. I pushed, lifted, pushed. The door was apparently locked.

I banged feebly against the door with my remaining strength, but in reality, it was probably nothing more than a tap. I tried screaming for help, but it was little more than a whisper, and that's when I must have passed out.

Georgina and I talked for what could have been five

minutes or five hours. She told me how much she'd loved me. I knew not to speak of adult love and imagined that she probably just admired me. But maybe she was in love with the thought of me, as I was with her, or him, at that time.

As I lay in a puddle of twisted limbs and crumpled clothing, Georgina stroked my hair and told me she'd styled herself on me, that I'd been her inspiration. I confessed that she'd…they'd been the one that allowed me to understand I was gay.

I'm not sure she understood, so I changed the subject. I asked her about her mother and Georgina explained she never got angry, but she liked everything to be a certain way and told him when he was getting it wrong. I could feel her becoming upset again and changed the subject back to talking about clothes and hair and the happiness that comes from reading.

*

It was an unwelcome jolt. The door opened and I tumbled out. Donald stood in front of me. 'As I remember,' he said, 'I found you here the last time, and I'd thought I'd made myself quite clear, that I didn't want you to come back to Deauville.'

I was still groggy, but I knew I had to get out of the house as quickly as possible, and saying anything in my state wouldn't be clever.

'I've called Mary,' Donald said. 'She's waiting at the front door.'

I was halfway down the main staircase, Donald one step ahead of me, no doubt ready to catch me. Then I remembered the diary.

I ran back up and, well-practised now, retrieved Georgina's diary from its hiding place. I hid it underneath my jumper and headed back down the stairs, pushing past Donald. I was out into the sunshine before Donald or Hilary could say anything.

As I flung myself into Mary's arms, I vowed to carry out Georgina's final wishes. I would burn her diary that very night, with all its pain and secrets.

Acknowledgements

Loanna Fychan for her dedicated editing services.

Caden de Grey my literary agent. Thanks for going the extra mile.

Unchained Pen for their bravery and determination to launch my writing career.

Thanks to my three mums, Rowan, Averylle and Caitlin, and Dad, Llywelyn ap Gruffudd, the last king of Wales, for launching my existence.

About the Author

For more on Foyle, see their Instagram account:
@foyle_ravenstead

Foyle resides at Foyle's Castle, St Dunstan, Isles of Sidhe. They are the benevolent leader of the Inner Council of the Isles of Sidhe.

An accomplished painter, poet, orator and statesperson, Foyle is also a keen snowboarder and alpine climber.

If you've enjoyed reading this story, please leave a review on Amazon or Goodreads.

Printed in Great Britain
by Amazon

46561930R00121